Stephen Hanson

Cover :
Adolphe Appia, Rhythmic Space – *Scherzo,* 1909
(Collection suisse du théâtre, Bern)

Revised edition, published by Pro Helvetia—Arts Council of Switzerland, 1982.

Printed by Grafiheld, Renens/Lausanne, Switzerland.

Adolphe Appia
1862–1928
actor – space – light

exhibition produced by
Pro Helvetia—Arts Council
of Switzerland

designed by
Denis Bablet and
Marie-Louise Bablet

John Calder (Publishers) Ltd, London
Riverrun Press, New York

The exhibition was produced by PRO HELVETIA—Arts Council of Switzerland.

The exhibition itself, the audio-visual displays, and the catalogue were planned by DENIS BABLET (Paris) and MARIE-LOUISE BABLET (Geneva).
Denis Bablet holds the rank of «directeur de recherche» at the French National Center for Scientific Research, where he is in charge of the group for theatrical and musicological research. Marie-Louise Bablet is in charge of the edition of Adolphe Appia's collected works currently being prepared by the Swiss Theatre Society with the help of the Swiss National Fund for Scientific Research.

HARRY ZAUGG (Bern) was responsible for the graphic design of the exhibition and its technical execution.
Harry Zaugg is a set-designer ; he is in charge of exhibition at the Bern Historical Museum.

Reconstruction of designer's models for stage sets : Harry Zaugg, assisted by Stefan Rebsamen and Greth Schmalzl (Bern).

Photographic reproduction : Stefan Rebsamen (Bern).

The English translation of the catalogue was done by Burton Melnick (Geneva).

Coordination for the production of the exhibition and for the editing and revision of the catalogue : Irène Lambelet, Pro Helvetia.

The exhibition was awarded the SPECIAL PRIZE OF THE JURY at the 1979 Prague Quadrennial for Scenography.

Pro Helvetia would like to thank all those institutions and officials who made photographs or original works available, and so made this exhibition possible.

Switzerland :

> Collection suisse du théâtre, Bern ; Martin Dreier
> Société suisse du théâtre, Bern ; Karl Gotthilf Kachler, Lydia Benz-Burger
> Musée d'art et d'histoire, Geneva ; Claude Lapaire
> Gabriel Jaques-Dalcroze, Geneva
> Institut Jaques-Dalcroze, Geneva ; Dominique Porte, Marguerite Croptier
> Grand Théâtre de Genève ; Jean-Claude Riber

Federal Republic of Germany :

> Institut für Theaterwissenschaft an der Universität Köln ; Helmut Grosse
> Theatermuseum, Munich ; Ekehart Nölle
> Richard Wagner Museum, Bayreuth ; Manfred Eger
> Festspielhaus, Bayreuth ; Oswald Georg Bauer

France :

> Bibliothèque Nationale, Paris (Département Arts du Spectacle) ; Cécile Gitteaux

Pro Helvetia would also like to thank all those private individuals who contributed invaluable assistance.

Contents

Appia and theatrical space
From revolt to utopia

by Denis Bablet

How is space to be experienced? How are we to conceptualize and structure it? How is space to be represented? Each age, civilization, or society has set its answers to these questions into its own cultural framework and way of life. It etched them, so to speak, into its own self-image and into the image of itself it passed on to posterity.

The problem of space is not, however, an abstract one that arises outside of us. It arises, on the contrary, from the set of natural and inevitable relations that we have with it. On both the representational and structural levels, these relations—which man himself creates—allow mankind to give form to its symbols and myths, its beliefs and ideologies.

There are periods when the problem of experiencing, structuring, and representing space takes on a special keenness. At these times dramatic upheavals, which have been long in the making, finally occur; far from being isolated events, they fit into a whole pattern of disruptions having equally important effects in the political, social, and economic spheres. These deep-seated shifts of sensibility inevitably bring about a change in man's way of seeing and looking. It is not so much a question of man's passive perception of the world as it is of the vision that he actively projects onto it. More than by anything else, that projection is expressed—at the same time that it is effected—by the work of art.

The Renaissance was one of those periods of crystallization. Another was the end of the nineteenth century —at which time the transformation was particularly apparent in the plastic and graphic arts, in architecture and in the theatre.

In 1888, at the age of twenty-six, Adolphe Appia took the conscious decision to work at "reforming stage-directing". Let us look at the situation in the theatre at that time.

Two symbols come immediately to mind.

In Paris, thirteen years previously, the Opera, that "Temple" of art and pleasure, had been inaugurated with great pomp and ceremony. Located half-way between the temple of technical progress—the Gare Saint-Lazare—and the temple of money—the Bourse—the Paris Opera was the temple of music, but even more of fashionable entertainment. Designed for the Second Empire, it was in fact to serve the Third Republic (not to mention the Fourth and Fifth). No unified space was to be found there—not in any way, shape, or form; on the contrary, the separation of spaces was taken to the utmost limits of refinement. On the one hand, there were the sections meant for the audience, reflecting, in their very decoration, the organization of society along strict hierarchical lines—not only the lobbies but also the great central staircase, the ultimate fashionable locations where one went to be seen to advantage. The auditorium itself was strictly divided into orchestra, boxes, and balconies. In that immense, horse-shoe shaped, well-upholstered parlor the opera-glasses were aimed not only at the stage but also at the faces of the audience—not to say at the low-cut gowns and fashionable outfits of the ladies. Look at Renoir's painting *La Loge*. The picture dates from 1874, but the man and woman Renoir paints might have been portrayed at the inauguration of the Paris Opera. And on the other hand, there was the stage, an immense empty space rising above its infrastructure and overhung by the flies—a veritable factory for theatrical images with its traditional machinery cleverly camouflaged. This was not yet the era of functionalism. The sole interface between house and stage was the proscenium, pierced by a kind of gigantic keyhole—the proscenium arch—and cut off from view by a highly ornamented curtain in which red and gold predominated.

The Paris Opera thus represented the fruition and triumph of the Italian type stage, the structures of which were here brought to their final degree of perfection. In the Paris Opera the Italian style theatre enjoyed its moment of supreme glory before being called fundamentally into question.

The year 1875 saw the inauguration of the Paris Opera, 1876 the opening of the Bayreuth Festspielhaus, designed according to the conceptions of Richard Wagner. Here was a new "model" of theatrical architecture destined, right up to the present day, to be imitated throughout the world. Was it, however, really so very revolutionary? The auditorium was, to be sure. Laid out in a unified space inspired by the Greco-Roman theatre was a vast bank of tiered seats, which, since privileges were done away with and visibility was the same for everyone, was apparently intended to create equality among the members of the audience. But the stage itself, huge and deep, retained both proscenium arch and curtain ; the disappearance of the orchestra into its "mystic abyss" did not change a thing so far as the stage was concerned. Not only did stage and auditorium remain separate—everything worked to make the stage even more distant, so as to reinforce illusion and therby magnify the heroic world on stage. Here, then, we find revolutionary development in the auditorium but traditionalism on stage and in the relation between the auditorium and the stage.

How did the stages of these two "Temples" of music "function"? There were a good many stylistic differences between Rubé and Chaperon, set-designers at the Paris Opera, and Hoffmann and the Brückners, who worked at Bayreuth. But in fact—once we go beyond the surface—the actual bases of set design were the same in Paris and on the "sacred hill" of Bayreuth. Space was subject to bald gimmickry. No matter that the techniques of trompe-l'œil and aerial and linear perspective were practiced by virtuosi. Shaky flats hung at various levels of the stage in catch-as-catch-can conjunction with heavy, esthetically dubious platforms. The whole jarred with the wooden boards and immutable flatness of the stage floor. And what a difference there was between the designer's sketch of the set—pure dream—and its execution !

The visual chaos of overloaded sets carried the day. The audience's attention was dispersed by the accumulation of pseudo-historical detail by which the general impression—and the drama itself—were swamped.

The actor appeared as an intruder for whom the stage space was not truly intended. The stage was a container for illusions, a box in which singers and actors breathed their rarefied air as they moved *in front* of an apparently three-dimensional picture—a background that smothered them—rather than *in* a set truly created for their movements. There was no harmony among the various means of dramatic and visual expression, and no real definition. As for the Wagnerian dream of the *Gesamtkunstwerk* or "total work of art," it simply disappeared, or else became merely an unattainable ideal always out of reach. "Ah, I abhor these costumes and this greasepaint," said Wagner. He added, "I created the invisible orchestra ; now if only I could invent the invisible theatre !"

Appia's reaction to this situation was complex. He reacted, to be sure, against the piling on of naturalistic detail, but even more against the very idea of trying to recreate the real scene of the action through naturalistic illusion. His reason was not only that "giving the illusion of reality is the negation of art," but also that any such illusion was impossible. In the first place, the powerful electric lighting that had recently been developed for the theatre revealed that what one had imagined to be branches with their autumn foliage or awesome boulders was in fact only painting on canvas. Furthermore, no harmonization was possible between trompe-l'œil painting on canvas and the three-dimensional reality of the actor's body. Moreover, any attempt at creating so impossible a harmony could lead only to dissociating the human body from the background provided for it by the set. Illusion could not come, therefore, from the pictorial images of the stage-set, but only from the living, radiant presence of the actor—the vital element in the creation of theatrical space. To achieve this sort of illusion, however, the visual and spatial chaos that caused such disastrous dissonance between the musical drama itself and the visual form that productions of it took had to be done away with ; it needed to be replaced by some ordered arrangement—one that would bring out the deep spiritual harmony of the drama and allow it to come to fulfillment in the newly purified air of the stage.

Appia's mission was to straighten things out, to replace the coexistence of conflicting elements with a functional arrangement that drew its expressive power from the hierarchical ordering of the means of theatrical expression. What is the art of staging but "the art of projecting into space what the dramatist was able to project only into time" ? From this, the whole texture of a theatrical performance can be defined. In Wagnerian drama and *Worttondrama* (music drama) generally, the music "regulates every element and group according to the necessities of the dramatic action." It thus dictates the actor's movements and actions, and thereby defines theatrical space. In the theatre, music is time, as real as it is ideal ; and through the actor it is metamorphosed into a kind of space at once spiritual and material—a kind of space, moreover, that can be embodied in a precise and decisive visual arrangement. Hence the famous hierarchy : actor – space – light – painting, in which light (as opposed to *signs)* is the expressive element. Light enlivens both space and actor—in their coexistence and mutual presence, in their opposition, and in their coming together. In this kind of space the relations between the actor and his body partake equally of collusion and antagonism ; the tension between the two works to enhance the expressive power of the human body that the actor has become. Now we can understand the advice Appia gave to his student Jessica Davis Van Wyck. (For all its appearance of being of only anecdotal interest, it is basic to Appia's thought.) "Show things with your legs," he told her, "and not with your eyes." If, as Pythagoras said, man is the measure of all things, the actor is the measure of theatrical space.

Appia, though, was not one to lock himself into a definitive theory or a vision established once and for all, although he did often remain faithful to certain images that welled up of themselves in his consciousness and emerged onto his drawing paper. Once on the paper, however, they remained subject to those famous erasures of his which eliminated everything superfluous in order to attain the essential—a simple diagram of the stage and its set. The organization of space that Appia was after left, as he saw it—as he *projected* it—less and less room for pictorial representation. From his first Wagnerian undertakings in the nineties to his late sketches of the twenties, Appia tended towards an increasingly rigorous simplicity, a sort of concrete abstraction in which the form mattered more than the object. It seems almost as if he sought to substitute a *spiritual* space for the *picturing* of space, to summon up something, born of music and the actor's movement, which could take its real form only in the spectator's mind.

From 1892 and 1896 on, Appia's sketches were, to be sure, revolutionary in their stylization ; but Appia went farther, into primary forms, timeless walls, staircases, slopes, on which the play of light and shadow anticipated the famous "rhythmic spaces" which he designed in 1909-10 for Jaques-Dalcroze. These "rhythmic spaces," he explained, were "meant for the enhancement of the human body governed by music." They were, to quote Appia again, pure "rhythmic geometry." (He coined the expression for the composition called *Scherzo*. Restrained and charged with mystery, it is one of-the most beautiful of the rhythmic spaces, though one of the least well known.)

Appia's theory and the determination with which he developed and applied it were supported, confirmed, and reinforced by experience ; all this was reflected in Appia's spiritual vision and the exemplary, quasi-ascetic self-discipline to which it gave rise. Also reflected in that vision and self-discipline, however, was the struggle of a tormented and extremely sensitive being to master himself and his own painful inner contradictions through the recreation of nature—or, better, through the creation of a new kind of nature. It was an artificial nature, true ; nevertheless it was a marvellously well-balanced one—in the articulation of its volumes, in the play of its light and shadow, in the sense of plenitude that pervaded its atmosphere, and in its opening onto the infinite. This artificial nature lived up to the real nature that Appia was intimate with, the one he was accustomed to see in its bare lines and primary elements : water, sky, walls, and light—the horizontality of the water of Lake Geneva, the verticality of a cypress tree, the play of verticals and horizontals in the vineyards of the canton of Vaud.

The space that Appia constructed was therefore a functional one in relation to the drama and the actor—it became a kind of launching pad for the actor's movements. But it was deeply expressive as well and, as Jaques-Dalcroze put it, "emotive." This was first of all because Appia envisioned the series of spatial levels that extends up the stage as a kind of expressive hierarchy—the more a character interacts with the "environment provided by the set," the more he takes part in external actions, whereas the more he removes himself from the set and approaches the audience, the more he is given over to the inner life and its expression. But Appia's space was expressive and "emotive" for another reason as well : by subjecting space to the will of shifting, moving light, Appia brought space alive. He gave space a life of its own, capable of touching us to our very depths. And there was nothing redundant about the expressivity that Appia gave to space ; it both blended and counterpointed with the other means of theatrical expression.

Appia did not stop there. From simplified forms he moved on to standardized forms : cubes, blocks, steps, screens. Here was the basic equipment for the Jaques-Dalcroze Institute in Hellerau—an equipment which, combined once again with light, held the potential for suggesting anything at all, and could potentially provide every possible means for reinforcing the expressivity of the human body. The expression "stage-setting" had lost its naturalistic connotations, for we were now in possession of a veritable set of building blocks that allowed us to set up simple arrangements on demand. The theatre thereby recovered its ludic power. At the same time it not only returned (like all the arts of the period) to the simplest and most classic "primal" shapes ; it also entered the age of variability and transformability.

As early as the period of the first sets he designed for Wagner, Appia had demonstrated the impossibility of reconciling the living, moving presence of the actor with the stolid impassivity of a frozen, lifeless set. Evidence for this is to be found in the series of sketches he made for the rocky site in Act II of The Valkyrie—sketches which show clouds coming and going, weighing down the atmosphere or liberating space. (Later, from the end of the century on, Appia called for the use of slides to convert this vision into theatrical reality.)

And Appia went further. Resolutely he broke up the immobility of stage space by adjusting the mobility of the elements of the set—the hangings in Lohengrin are an example—to the fluidity of the music. He thus did away with the breaks between scenes ; in so doing he both preserved temporal unity and—through the transformation of the temporal into the spatial—insured the spatial continuity of the drama. Appia's "kinetics of the stage," while less radical than Craig's or Svoboda's, occupies a determining position in the history of the theatre—and of art—in the twentieth century.

As radical as Appia's reforming—or transformation—of space was, however, he could not be satisfied with it so long as it affected only the "set" or the "stage." No man of the theatre who has given any thought to the matter believes that theatre can be reduced to the stage. If theatre is confined to the stage, it dies. A theatrical event is first and foremost an act, in which everyone participates in different ways. The place where this act occurs is one of receptivity, of contact, of living exchange ; from it, living expression arises. It was therefore normal and logical that Appia should turn his attention to the playhouse—to the theatrical *place*—in its totality, and that he should attempt to undo the dichotomy between auditorium and stage. His purpose was to bring the actor closer to the spectator and, eventually, to merge the two.

This was the end then of the irrevocable separation between stage and auditorium that came with the decadent Italian type theatre. Appia's tactics became fiercer as his strategy became more systematic ; at each new stage, Appia pressed further on. As the years pass most directors lose their youthful radicalism. Not so with Appia. On the contrary, his ideals became stronger, and from the growth of the demands he made, there followed not only a surpassing of himself but also a transcending of the theatre as it had been known.

Very early on Appia had rebelled against the barriers between auditorium and stage ; very early on he had decried the architecture that effected the separation : the proscenium arch—that ridiculous window that confines the stage picture—and the footlights—that "monstrosity," as he called it, of our theatre. A further stimulus to bringing the auditorium and the stage closer together came from his discovery of Eurythmics. Appia was the one who in 1908 suggested to the Morax brothers that they connect the auditorium and the conventional stage of the Théâtre populaire du Jorat in Mézières, Switzerland with a large stairway at the front of the stage. The inspiration for the spatial arrangement of the auditorium at the Jaques-Dalcroze Institute in Hellerau came from him. The relation of the onstage action to the spectators, who are gathered onto a single bank of tiered seats, remained frontal ; but both actors and audience were enclosed in the single, homogeneous atmosphere of a unified volume. Neither footlights nor proscenium arch separated the auditorium from the vast surface of the acting area that extended right up to the first tier of seats, ready to receive whatever was constructed in the way of a set. Claudel, who produced his play *The Tidings Brought to Mary* there in 1913, was right to describe the Hellerau Institute as a "workshop." Hellerau exploded the usual limits of the theatre and headed towards a form of "experimental" theatre, both in what was put on and in the way space was structured. The Hellerau Institute prefigured Appia's stubborn dream of what he variously called "halls of syntheses," a "ground for experiment," a "touchstone for dramatic art." Nowhere was that dream better expressed than in the second preface to *Music and Stage-Directing.* Appia was writing in October, 1918, on the eve of the Armistice. Though he did not belong to one of the belligerent countries, he had felt the tragedy of the war keenly and had been deeply affected by it. His words merit careful attention ; already he saw the possibilities of reconciliation for mankind at large and for society. In the following words he envisions the theatre of the future—but more than theatre in the narrow sense, he envisions a *social act.*

"Little by little this term "performance" will become anachronistic, even meaningless. We will want to act with a single mind, by unanimous consent. The dramatic art of tomorrow will be a *social act* in which everyone will take part. And who knows, perhaps after a transitional period we will come to majestic celebrations in which a whole people will participate—in which each of us will express his feelings, his grief and his joy, and at which no one will any longer be willing to remain a passive spectator. *That* will be the playwright's triumph!"

And what of the playhouse? And what of space?

"Sooner or later we will come to what will be called the *hall,* the cathedral of the future, which, in a free, vast, and variable space, will play host to the most diverse activities of our social and artistic life. This will be the ultimate setting for dramatic art to flourish in—*with or without spectators.*"

What better expression can there be of Appia's idealism—of the aspiration of that forever solitary spirit towards an ideal of artistic communalism that would release the creativity of body and spirit and bring both into total harmony? To be sure, there is probably something dangerous about Appia's utopia—as there is in the term "cathedral of the future," which possibly implies replacing the worship of a dead god with that of a human community celebrating itself in its own self-expression.

There is, however, no denying that in those few forthright lines Appia expressed not only the most radical revolution of our century concerning the place and space in which theatre occurs but also an aspiration which has been much repeated since his time : that of the right to creation for everyone.

My title is *Appia and Theatrical Space.* Was *From Revolt to Utopia* the right sub-title? Might I not have said quite simply *From Yesterday to Today?*

For look at all those around us who are at work breaking up and exploding traditional space and bringing the actor and the spectator closer together mentally and physically ; all of them—often without realizing it—owe to Appia just as much as contemporary painters owe to Cézanne, the cubists, and the first abstract artists.

Denis Bablet

Appia as he saw himself

Genève - 24 - 11 - 15

Toujours avec vous ! vous le savez — mais
j'aime à vous le répéter . Je viens de passer 10 jours
chez les Jaques-Dalcroze — et, par conséquent, à
l'Institut de Dalcroze . — Si bien — simple —
pédagogique — et où les élèves se sentent heureux
d'abord — et chez eux ensuite — .

Combien souvent j'y pensais à vous ! à ce que
je souhaiterais que nous puissions ensemble, vous qui
représentez si bien ce que je ne suis pas, hélas ; moi
qui cherche de toute mon âme à être et à développer
ce que vous ne savez pas être . Ainsi, nous serions
non seulement ensemble — mais nous serions Un.
Que les échos de Copeau m'ont intéressé et

The period of creation... preceded the period of theoretical reflection ; that order seems to me to have insured the artistic integrity of my vision of the stage. First I saw... inside myself—but with perfect clarity ; then and only then (that is the essential point) did I reflect theoretically on the value and appropriateness of what I saw.

From *Introduction to My Personal Notes,*
unpublished manuscript, 1905.

Thank you for your kind and affectionate letter. I am always very touched that you should feel any solicitude for me, for if my mind has the good fortune to live in my ———⋚———— Elysian Fields, the rest of my being is not so lucky. I can't complain, though, since solitude is necessary to me and since, materially, I like simplicity. Also, traveling is not desirable at present.

My character and temperament do not allow me the *active* life that my artistic faculties would seem to call for. I work well only when I work alone ; that is a fate I've gotten used to.

Excerpt from an unpublished letter to
Edward Gordon Craig, January 31, 1919.

fait du bien ! Il paraît si bien vous comprendre ! —
Dans 4 ou 5 jours je serai de retour à
Glérolles, — Glérolles où vous seriez heureux,
je crois — et moi avec vous.

Ne cessez pas de m'écrire, ainsi que vous le
faites, vos petits mots de présence ... — j'en ai
besoin.

Je pense à vous et vous aime par toutes les
attaches qui nous lient indissolublement et
qui sont si vraies, si fortes — si légères quand
même —

votre Adolphe Appia

Unpublished letter from Adolphe Appia to Gordon Craig, November 24, 1915.
(Collection Gordon Craig, Bibliothèque Nationale, Département Arts du spectacle, Paris.)

Appia as seen by

Jacques Copeau, Edward Gordon Craig, Vsevolod Meyerhold, Firmin Gémier, Emile Jaques-Dalcroze, Serge Volkonski

Jacques Copeau :

Every time I went to Switzerland to give a series of performances, my old friend would come out of retirement to meet us in Geneva or Lausanne. With my actors he had established a sort of paternal cameraderie, which was full of grace and of a noble kind of familiarity. He used to call them "children." "I respect those children," he would say. Appia was the ideal spectator. Nothing escaped him, either in the actors' performances or in the details of the directing. All the dramatic action reached him not only through his mind but through his body. After the show he would tell us how we had acted. He would repeat all of our gestures. His big white teeth would light up his smile. His eyes—he had admirable ones—would send out flashes of lightning. And if anything was as great as his capacity for enthusiasm, it was his courtesy. He never neglected anyone. He looked at everyone with the same attention and intensity. For him, every human being mattered.

When Appia's health no longer allowed him to go out, I would go to Nyon. In the midst of spacious grounds stood a modest little house. On the second floor was a small room with a metal bed, a table, and a few chairs. That is where Appia lived with his pencils, his manuscripts, his drawings, and a small number of books— Rabelais, Molière, Shakespeare. For a long time he had no longer needed the scores of Wagner's operas— he knew them *all* by heart. Outside the window a great tree swayed in the breeze. Today, at the foot of that tree are buried the ashes of a heart that adored life and beat only for beauty. There was no pomp at Appia's funeral. He did not want anyone to be disturbed. His will is penciled onto half a page—Appia always wrote in pencil—above a firm, slender signature. It bequeathes the posthumous care of his work to three friends who will be able to be of service to it. Those few lines, like all those that Appia wrote or drew throughout his life, reflect his natural nobility and a great inner calm...

I made his acquaintance nearly fifteen years ago, at Glérolles on Lake Geneva, where Dalcroze had taken me to meet him. Adolphe Appia was already that magnificent, cheerful, solitary gentleman in whose presence I was to spend so many unforgettable hours. He had a long gray beard ; a high and singularly powerful head topped by a snowy shock of hair ; wide, sparkling eyes that were always a little moist ; and a sensual mouth from which speech emerged hesitantly—sometimes in cooing tones, sometimes explosively. Appia had a slight stutter. And this impediment no doubt added a further feeling of apprehension to his native shyness. Although he liked company and was happy to be liked by others, and although in friendship as in art, as he used to say, he had a need for genuine human presence, he was often chary of contact with the world. He would on occasion brusquely call off a visit or an interview, or would, for no apparent reason, walk out of a meeting or a theatre—in order to go outside, to breathe freely. His nervous sensitiveness was extreme. That is why he did so little actual onstage work. Not only any compromise but the slightest contact with contin- gencies, the slightest need to fit his principles to circumstances, was intolerable to him. And we ought not to complain of this or to reproach Appia for it, nor ought we to see in this abstention of his any lessening of his genius. On the contrary, Appia might well have lessened his genius by trying to overcome this block in his character. "Alas," he wrote me, "I am not made for direct action, and have to take refuge in the lead of my pencil." He did enough for us with that pencil for us not to have to ask him for more. His mind achieved its fulfillment and power only in those areas in which the petty resistances of our profession do not arise. The discoveries he made are real ones. As he liked to say, they put solid ground under his feet. The reality of the stage that lived in him was more alive than what we see in the theatre. And he did not in the least look down on attempts that were less ambitious or more limited than his own. He admired the *heroism* of certain men of the theatre who were willing to make the most of circumstances. One felt modesty in him and never pride. Ugliness in the theatre, or baseness, or ostentatious virtuosity, or banality made him *blush.* He shuddered at working backstage. He worked outdoors, while walking, by the lake or in the forest. I can still see him as he was when he came to meet me in Glérolles : tall, erect, easy. He held his head high ; his stride was graceful ; his fine legs were encased in tight-fitting woolen stockings ; and his whole figure stood out against the curtain of yellow gold that the autumn vineyards made behind him.

Appia's first and greatest merit—which he shares with Craig—is this : he broke out of the theatre and took us with him. He denied and repudiated the theatre—but out of love for that living art. He replanted it and allowed it to take root elsewhere than between the dusty boards of a stage that had become debased. He punched a hole in the ceiling of that box-like container for second-rate marvels ; air came in, and we saw the sky. As life returned, the ideas of greatness and style became clear to us ; in order to serve them we have returned to the eternal verities.

Excerpts from "Adolphe Appia and the Art of the Stage" ("Adolphe Appia et l'art scénique") in *La Nación,* Buenos Aires, April 16, 1928.

SCHOOL FOR THE ART OF THE THEATRE.
ARENA GOLDONI. VIA DEI SERRAGLI 101
FLORENCE - ITALY.
DIRECTOR: E. GORDON CRAIG

Friday.

I have your picture (photograph) in front of my desk always. And the more I see it the more beautiful it seems to me. (a banal-true thing to say.)

It excites me far more than any other artwork which belongs to our age.
There is no escape from it & one wishes not to escape because it gives NO OFFENCE.
But how inviting it is - how gracious - how silent - how perfectly temperate - how G O O D -

Excerpt from an unpublished letter from Gordon Craig to Adolphe Appia, May 4, 1914. (Collection suisse du théâtre, Bern)

Edward Gordon Craig :

Friday

I have your picture (photograph)
in front of my desk always.
And the more I see it
the more beautiful it seems to me.

(a banal-true thing to say.)

It excites me far more than any other artwork which belongs to our age.

There is no escape from it & one wishes not to escape because it gives NO OFFENCE.

But *how* inviting it is – how gracious – how silent – how perfectly temperate – how G O O D.

Firmin Gémier :

I am expecting Appia to come to Paris with his model stage-settings. I want a triumph for him and for his ideas.

Excerpt from an undated letter from Gémier to Emile Jaques-Dalcroze.

Emile Jaques-Dalcroze :

I am deeply impressed with the beauty, simplicity, and power of your conception ; I have never seen or known spaces that were more rhythmic or more evocative of rhythms.

My whole-hearted thanks for having shown me your masterpieces. I cannot express the deep feeling that the sight of them brought ; let me simply state that it is the most beautiful music I have ever heard.

You have a contemplative, imaginative, intuitive character. You need real, material experiences in the realm of the plastic. Like me, you suffer the advantage of being able to execute your will immediately.

My dear friend,

Thank you for your good advice. You are right a thousand times over. For training exercises those movable elements are invaluable to me—they allow us to discover new postures in new conditions of balance. But from the artistic point of view—so long as light has not come into play—the feeling of life is definitely missing and those constructions of levels and planes seem mere skeletons or mummies.

My dear friend,   15 August

I have just come back to the Institute and found your drawings. They take hold of me over and over again. I get unwound from them, then all wound up again. They show me the immediate relations between plastic, musical gestures and my educational and esthetic wishes. Yes, we are together—my dear, dear friend !

                                                                             Christmas

And then there is you, who are the true musician—he who can situate emotion in space and make space emotive. That is everything.

Excerpts from undated letters written to
Adolphe Appia by Jaques-Dalcroze between 1908 and 1916.

Serge Volkonski :

The first and most important thing that strikes us when we look at Appia's designs is the horizon. The most "distant" thing on earth is the maritime horizon, where sky and water meet. There is no limit to what one senses, no end to what one supposes. The horizon is—in the realm of the possible, of course—the most physical expression of the infinite and hence the visual expression of eternity.

I pictured that meeting in my mind's eye. I saw the Englishman's graying blond mane over his baby-pink face, and I visualized the tousled black hair that topped the manly, sun-tanned forehead of the Swiss. I heard the hurried, vivacious talk of the one, the shy, stuttering talk of the other. One was a sparkling fountain, in which speech almost preceded thought, and the other was penetration in depth, deeply felt but barely expressed. With his eccentric gestures the refined Englishman—a playful esthete and a philosopher with a predilection for the paradoxical—drew highly imaginative pictures of nonexistent worlds ; and at the same time the Swiss—a son of the forests, coarse but sensitive, mumbling but persuasive—was speaking with a burning look of the recognition of art and life thanks to the brilliant discovery of Jaques-Dalcroze.

In spite of myself, I wondered where the true task lay that would be worthy of an artist : to take man out of real life, towards the imaginary world of stories, or else to bring that imaginary world into human life.

Excerpts from "Appia and Craig," in *Khudojestvennye otkliki,* Saint Petersburg, 1912.

Vsevolod Meyerhold :

Drawing his inspiration from the heart of music, the composer of a musical drama uses words and musical sound to bring to life a concrete image of his creation ; thus the score comes into being—a text woven of words and music.

Appia (in *Music and Stage-Directing*) considers it impossible to approach any dramatic conception otherwise than by first plunging into the world of the emotions, in the musical sphere.

Appia holds it for impossible to proceed directly ; any dramatic conception that has not worked its way through music will lead to a poor libretto.

Here, moreover, is how he defines the reciprocal relations among the elements of opera :

From *music*
in the broad sense of the word
arises
the dramatic conception

Production of the drama in time	This conception is developed in images through words and notes into a drama This drama becomes visible to the audience with the help	in the score
Production of the drama in space	of the actor of volumes of lighting of painting Thus the *Worttondrama* comes into being	in the staging

The music, which determines the duration of everything that happens on stage, gives a rhythm which has no relation to the everyday world. The life of music is not that of everyday reality. "Neither life as it is nor life as it should be, but life as it is seen in dreams" (Chekhov).

The whole essence of stage rhythm is poles apart from that of reality and everyday life.

That is why the whole appearance of the actor on stage should be that of an artistic fiction. This fiction may no doubt sometimes be rooted in a realistic ground, but in the last analysis it is to be presented in a way that is very far removed from what we see in real life. There should be a *symmetry* between the actor's movements and gestures and the stylized character of the dialogue he sings.

In naturalistic drama, the actor's control comes from the observation of life and the transferal into his acting of the results of that observation ; in music drama the actor's control must be subjected to more than just the experience of life.

Indeed, in naturalistic drama the actor's control often finds itself subject to the arbitrariness of his temperament. The actor in music drama, however, is freed from the arbitrariness of personal temperament by the score, which sets a fixed meter.

The actor in music drama must grasp the essence of the score and translate all the subtleties in what the orchestra has expressed into a language of plastic expression.

Control of his own physical suppleness is thus a sine qua non for the actor in music drama.

The human body, with its suppleness and mobility, is now one of the "means of expression," like the orchestra and the set, and has begun to play an active role in the whole dramatic movement.

Man and set now share a mutual harmony ; man and music now share a mutual rhythm. Like the set and music, *man* himself is becoming a *work of art.*

Excerpts from "The Staging of *Tristan and Isolde* at the Marinski Theatre—October 30, 1909." (Published in *Ecrits sur le Théâtre,* tome 1, La Cité, Lausanne, 1973.)

Adolphe Appia
Fragments from a life's work

A LOOK AT THE PAST AND THE FUTURE

The second preface to
Music and Stage-Directing

At the period when the author wrote and published this volume, the problem of stage-directing—and therefore of dramatic art—never came up. The only type of innovation that either the audience or professionals of the theatre were concerned about consisted in an increasing sumptuousness of ornamental detail or a continually refined realism. That conception of staging doomed the playwright to merely marking time. The only really promising attempt at reform at that time was to be found in the exceptional nature of the productions and of the auditorium (as opposed to the stage) at Bayreuth. On the far side of the curtain, however, the *stage* at Bayreuth offered nothing that in any way corresponded to the marvels of the score. On account of this painful contrast and the perpetual repetition of this perpetually re-arising conflict, the work accomplished at Bayreuth gave rise to a highly fecund artistic revolt. This is why Wagner's work will always remain inseparable from the reformation of the stage and of drama in general that is now in course.

From *Music and Stage-Directing (La Musique et la mise en scène*, Theaterkultur-Verlag, Bern 1963).

RICHARD WAGNER, THE STARTING POINT FOR APPIA'S THOUGHT

The Staging of Wagnerian Drama
"Preliminary Ideas"

Music, being time, sets the proportions. Thus the staging of Wagnerian drama has no need to take its examples of time-span from life. On the contrary, all the life it contains is rigorously set by the drama itself. Hence this type of drama falls *in its entirety* on the shoulders of the playwright-composer, who in a sense creates both time and space. When the means in his possession are adequate to justify his creation, he wields the greatest evocative power that exists. The dramas of Richard Wagner do not meet this condition, and yet they are the only ones of this new type that we possess. Today's conditions for this type of art-work are not, therefore, the normal ones. If we nevertheless wish to convince the audience of the original life that these dramas do contain, the manner of presenting them becomes a highly delicate matter. Now, it so happens that the conditions the audience imposes are in agreement with the basic condition of Wagnerian drama—i.e., that we are to find life only *within* the drama. Thus the director of Wagner's dramas will have to let himself be guided exclusively—and servilely—by everything that the drama he wishes to stage reveals to him of its own life.

In establishing in the abstract the conditions for his drama, Wagner, therefore, tacitly established the conditions for staging it, since the latter are necessarily contained in the former. Only in the application that he made of those conditions did he neglect to follow out the consequences rigorously.

"The form of stage production"

Our remarks must at present limit themselves to Wagner's dramas. Although their author set them in today's conditions of production, those conditions, as we have seen, are incapable of providing the required intensity—they are, that is to say, inadequate to the life of the drama. The life of the drama is given by music. In order to be able to counterpose to it analogous means of staging, it remains for us to see just what the nature of musical intensity is from the point of view of stage production.

Up until now the actor has moved independently in an inanimate picture ; he could not in any way merge with it. The dramatic action set the picture imprecisely, and the actor was connected to it only by the material necessities of his role. As it was impossible to suppose the existence of any element that could bring the two into harmony, attempts were made to bridge the gap through what might be suggested by the action—and even to subordinate the action to the possibilities of stage production. But we rapidly wearied of experiments in staging ; the drama then appeared in all its insignificance—or else revealed itself to be independent of the means for stage production that had been considered an integral part of it. It could only turn into some more or less living picture, or else slip back into one of its earlier forms. The need to connect the actor to the inanimate picture was not of sufficient concern to justify all those efforts ; indeed, that need interfered with the action, on account of the lack of any means which could express an actual merging between the two elements (rather than merely the need for such a merging).

Wagner solved the problem. Wherever the drama requires the merging of the elements involved in production, the playwright-composer finds the means in music. What we had been seeking to bring about by choosing a dramatic action that was adapted to the possibilities of staging exists, then, in Wagnerian drama from the very beginning. Far from limiting the action, it gives it the possibility of inexhaustible variety.

As far as stage production is concerned, the essence of musical intensity is that *the music should govern all the elements involved in production and group them according to the necessities of the dramatic action*——so that the performance takes on a flexibility that will allow it to pay unconditional obedience to the musical requirements. Since we are dealing here with a matter of proportions, all that remains for us to do is to examine the elements of theatrical technique and to subordinate them one to another in a way corresponding to the playwright-composer's means of expression.

The inanimate picture is made up of painting, spatial arrangement (i. e., the way in which the parts of the setting are laid out), and lighting. Spatial arrangement mediates between painting and lighting, just as lighting mediates between the two other means and the actor.

Even a novice in questions of stage-setting will understand that painting and lighting are mutually exclusive. For lighting up a vertical flat means simply making it visible, and has nothing to do with—indeed, is in opposition to—the active role of light. Spatial arrangement, on the other hand, works against painting, but can give efficient service to lighting. With regard to the actor, painting is completely subordinated to lighting and spatial arrangement.

The least necessary element in production is, therefore, painting ; and it is hardly necessary to prove that—if we leave aside the actor—lighting takes first place. Which of these elements is subject to the narrowest conventions? Painting is, without question, since spatial arrangement imposes substantial limitations on it, and since the active role played by lighting tends to exclude it altogether. Lighting, on the contrary, might be considered almighty, were it not for its dialectical contrary, painting, which perverts the use made of it. The importance of spatial arrangement depends on the other two elements ; that importance is limited or increased in direct proportion to the importance given to painting or lighting.

Painting, then, the least necessary element, interferes to a considerable extent with the development of the other two elements, which are of a higher order than it is. These paradoxical relationships obviously originate in the very conception of the form of stage production.

No one will deny that it will never lead anywhere to take staging as an end in itself ; we can, therefore, leave any such consideration out of our reasoning.

The form of a production is given by the form of the drama. More precisely, the audience tacitly imposes the external form it requires to be convinced of the life of the drama. The essential purpose of painting is to show what neither the actor nor lighting nor spatial arrangement can make visible. If painting has developed disproportionately, the reason is that the audience needed indications that painting alone could provide. In other words, painting was a condition posed by the existing dramatic forms. We have seen that the means of bringing about the merging of the actor and the inanimate picture did not exist until the creation of Wagnerian drama. Up until then staging needed to be loaded down with mutually complementary details that gave rise to the suggestion that the drama required. Similarly, since the author was unable to express the inner drama, he limited himself to indicating it through onstage action. The drama itself and its production were thus adequate to each other. Both were impotent to express the *fact,* and were obliged merely to indicate it, the one through the outward manifestations of life, the other through inanimate signs. Since painting was particularly well suited to providing these signs, it took on great importance, and came to use spatial arrangement, and then lighting, for its own purposes. The audience became used to doing the "translation" requi-red by the vertical flats and the absence of *active* light. It came to like seeing life presented through signs, and the use of those signs, when skilfully managed, did allow a very great freedom of choice. To the artificial need to see things "shown," the audience sacrificed much that was attractive—but above all it sacrificed the genuine life that lighting and spatial arrangement alone can give.

In bringing about the merging of all the elements, Wagnerian drama revealed the impotence of this concep-tion of the form of stage production. If Wagner set his own dramas into that form, it is nevertheless undeni-able that in such a form his work is totally incapable of revealing the life it contains.

The means of expression that today's dramatists have at their command through the use of poetic and musi-cal notation have attained their greatest power in the dramas of Wagner. Wagner made this possible by bringing those means of expression into a hierarchical arrangement, in which some are subordinated to others. The same should be done with the means of stage production. Let us look carefully at the hierarchical relationships that this process of arrangement and subordination will bring about.

Staging today puts all the means at its disposal in service to the *sign,* which receives its main support from painting. But since painting is the most disturbing and least expressive element, we should from the outset subordinate it to its dialectical contrary, lighting. We have seen that spatial arrangement mediates between and reconciles painting and lighting. The essential part of spatial arrangement consists in combining mov-able elements and platforms into a functional "core structure." Now, that "core structure" is dictated and determined by the actor and the requirements of his role. But for his part, the actor in Wagnerian drama possesses no freedom of initiative, since his entire role is set into the proportions given by the music—which is the very soul of the drama. In the last analysis, then, the drama determines the staging. But we must bear in mind above all that the drama can determine the staging only by going through the actor.

The life imposed on the actor by music differs from the life he needs to find for non-musical drama. In musical drama, the time-spans are irrevocably set, and shape the performance in keeping with the dramatic inten-tion. Consequently any given role already contains not only its temporal but also its spatial proportions—the latter resulting from the former. The union between the inanimate picture and the actor thus exists—implicitly, in a latent state—prior to any performance. Since the spatial arrangement is determined by the actor, and since the actor's role exists only within the proportions set by the music, it follows that the spatial arrangement itself takes on a musical importance. It becomes, in Wagner, the equivalent of a role in the drama. We must therefore cease allowing scene-painting to come into play for its own sake. For that redu-ces the dramatic meaning of spatial arrangement to nothingness and allows scene-painting to monopolize the lighting solely for its own advantage—thus destroying the essential factors in staging and encumbering the stage picture with *signs,* of which Wagnerian drama has no need. If lighting, for its part, is to have a life of its own, it can not hope for any freedom of expression, for if it were free to express itself, it would have no purpose. And lighting and painting both can accomplish nothing without spatial arrangement, on which the actor imposes the proportions set by the drama. If spatial arrangement, in its turn, carries out its double mission—allowing the painting to exist in spite of the lighting and allowing the lighting to function in spite of the painting—we will thus obtain for the form of the production an organic totality corresponding to the organism of the drama in the abstract. And the modes of expression, in mutual subordination, will take on the desired flexibility[1].

It will be painful to sacrifice scene-painting, given the perfection it has attained. Will there be sufficient compensations for this sacrifice in the advantages that will come from the new role played by lighting? Let us not forget that in its mediating role between the actor on one hand and spatial arrangement and painting on the other, lighting is, of all the elements of staging, the most important one for blending and merging. What we lose as far as the quantitative importance of the sign (i. e., painting) is concerned is restored to us by the vitality of direct expression. In order to fit the proportions set by the music, each element in a production will be able to provide the exact measure of expression required—and such flexibility will be possible only through the collaboration of the other elements.

Moreover, it would be a mistake to overestimate the extent of the sacrifice I have been discussing. For as scene-painting loses its independence, it will probably discover in its new set of relationships a purer source of invention than the one responsible for its current "fortunes." If the drama should sometimes call for it to take on a life of its own once more, it would comply, thoroughly aware of its true condition—and the audience for its part would not let itself be taken in by the brilliant appearances produced by scene-painting, in which it would see merely a dramatic necessity[2].

Viewed in this way, the inanimate picture exists only through the actor, who, as the intermediary between the drama itself and the form of the stage setting, predetermines that form in such a way that he can become part of it. His position is thus transformed. No longer does the author give him a role to create ; the role is imposed on him, already living and breathing with its own definitively established life. All the actor has to do is to take hold of that life. If it is true that in spoken drama the actor sometimes has to give up his own personality in order to enter into his role of the moment, that role nevertheless remains to a great extent his property ; the audience is so aware of that that it is often more concerned with the success of the actor and his

1) Staging itself can attain the rank of a *means of expression* only in a Wagnerian drama—a work of art which absorbs all of our faculties and makes it impossible for any one factor of the staging to stray from the totality or to extend over an undetermined space. Here, staging is no longer a mere material statement of circumstances, as it was formerly ; consequently, *illusion is not its purpose.* In *Tristan,* for example, the staging should be reduced to so strict a minimum that there can be no question of illusion. *The Mastersingers,* on the other hand, needs as much realistic life as possible.

2) See, below, the case of *The Twilight of the Gods.*

for us. In a place like the Greco-Roman theatre, where the stage and the amphitheatre make up a single esthetic unit, the presence of our sorry modern audience is a meaningless barbarity—quite as barbarous as the director's patent desire to bring the marvellously "modified" relationships of Greek tragedy back to the relationships of "real objects" among themselves.

Here, however, let us pause. In the theatre this totality of connected parts includes light as well as the actor and the stage setting. "Systematically modifying" the interrelations among these parts implies being able to control each one of them. Daylight eludes our control completely. Open air staging is thus deprived of one of the most powerful means of expression[1] ; the esthetic balance among the parts is broken and the possibility for any "systematic modification" is thereby considerably lessened. It is likely that the Greeks were aware of this fact. This would explain certain of their "modifications" (which *to us* appear uncalled for) ; one of the purposes of those "modifications" was perhaps to bring the appearance ot the things that could be controlled and modified into adjustment with the element of light, which was intractable.

Here we have touched upon one of the central problems of staging today—*light ;* it is important for us to have a precise understanding of. it.

The dramatic work in its totality cannot escape Taine's definition. We need, therefore, to find the means to make each of its parts flexible and responsive. For its author, the written play—with or without music—already fits that description. But there remains the staging ; and the elements of staging are, in hierarchical order, as follows : the actor, the arrangement of the set, the lighting, the painting of the flats.

Even if we leave the actor the freedom required by the need for dramatic vitality and by the interest that resides in a personal interpretation, we will nevertheless always retain enough authority over him to keep him within that organically based hierarchy. The other three elements are interdependent ; light, however, possesses the advantage of being perfectly flexible and totally responsive, and that gives it a place in the very first rank among the means of expression (though after the actor).

The problem is this : how, in enclosed theatres, can we preserve the superiority of light in relation to the other parts of the staging ; and in open air theatres, how can we replace its all powerful expression ?

At issue, we see, is the deployment of the elements other than lighting, since in open air lighting eludes our control and on a closed stage it is amenable to our wishes.

1) There is no need to say that when we are dealing with art, the flukes of the barometer do not enter in.

If we analyze the constituent elements of modern staging, their mutual effects, their simultaneous operation (as managed at present) and the influence it has on the actor's performance as well as on the very conception of the dramatic action, we will understand why the supremacy of lighting still goes unrecognized, and then, perhaps, we will be able to base staging on a different use of our resources.

This analysis will necessarily lead us to the play itself in its relations (close and well-founded, or less so) with the staging. We will thus be able to determine the influence of the play itself on the elements of stage performance.

When *music* is an integral part of the drama, it "modifies" the time-structure profoundly. In musical drama that brings about—or ought to—just as profound a modification in the general appearance of a production. Furthermore, music, starting from simple recitative, allows expression to rise to nearly unbelievable intensity ; and this span in itself constitutes an esthetic "modification" of the highest value.

Considered from this point of view, music offers staging an inestimable stylizing power—probably the only power that can regularize performance once and for all (that is to say, strip it of the needless artifices that undermine the effect of the indispensable ones).

Between music and light there exists a mysterious relationship. "Apollo was not only the god of song, but also the god of light" (H. S. Chamberlain). Let us not put asunder what that divinity has joined together ; let us seek to be his servants.

II

Musical sound and light. Two elements which, from an esthetic viewpoint, defy analysis.

"Where the other arts say, 'That *means,*' music says, 'That *is*'" (Richard Wagner).

When forms and colors seek to express something, light says, "I *am ;* forms and colors will come into being only through me."

How are we to approach these all powerful elements? Who will help us join them in an indissoluble bond?

Some great musicians have never even... taken any notice of light ; great painters and sculptors have never taken notice of music. "But," it will be said, "what does that matter to us in the theatre? We ourselves possess the necessary technical means."

It seems to me on the contrary that we bear the guilt for this mutual indifference—and that it is important both to make light visible to the often inattentive eye of the musician, and to make music more accessible to the often recalcitrant ear of the artist. For only then will we be able to begin our campaign on staging.

It is a deep inner reason that keeps artists from the theatre. I hope they will not be offended if a respectful layman attempts to seek out its origin.

"Is it on account of the absence of art in the theatre?" No doubt ; and from that we all suffer. But there is much more.

The only works that the artist customarily beholds with any real enthusuasm—i. e., experiences *as* an artist—are those that require some personal activity on his part or some specific contribution from him. That is what we call "understanding a work of art." But our theatrical productions do everything in their power to make that contribution unnecessary, or even, quite simply, impossible. No doubt we as spectators must our-selves construct, moment by moment, the highly prized illusion of our sets, and this we do out of overindul-gent habit. But—is that the personal activity that is so dear to the artist?

Alas, it is not ; indeed, the very idea of that is repugnant to him. Now, our modern theatre requires nothing else of us—except, it is true, the most appalling passivity.

What can the artist do with a stage production of this sort? For what the artist wants is to *do* something, and the abhorrence that he feels for the theatre arises because the theatre frustrates his dearest wish—a wish for esthetic activity on the part of the beholder.

If we wish to bring light and musical sound back together, if we wish to reunite the vision of the artist with the expression of the musician, it is indispensable to come up with some way of deploying the resources of the stage so as to satisfy the artist's basic wish, and to find some musical form which cannot exist without that new deployment—and which, indeed, will serve as its expression.

At present, music, for its part, has taken off on an unregulated, not to say lunatic, process of developing its virtuosity. It is thus continually moving farther away from the integral rhythm of the human being—the very rhythm from which it originally proceeds.

Staging has done the same. Scene painting has become a kind of virtuoso display that shows hardly any concern for the presence of the actor.

Bringing these two art forms back together—as they are proposed to us at present—cannot, therefore, lead to harmony.

The artist ought—for his own sake—to desire the aliveness of musical sound ; and the musician ought to feel an urgent need for an artistic externalization of his art. When this relationship becomes a necessary one—and consequently an organic one—then from it will blossom the art that can reconcile light and musical sound.

Apollo will again live among us.

But what point of convergence is there in the same work of art for light and musical sound? We wish to unify the two for the work that is to come ; but how, working from general principles only (since experimentation is not yet possible), can we bring about that unification?

Rhythm closely connects the life of musical sound to the movements of our organism. Here, already, is one guidepost, one important link. Furthermore, for any expression of light, plastic forms are indispensable[1]. What remains to be done is to bring together the movements that rhythm transmits to our bodily organisms (those movements being the essence of music cast back into space) and the plastic forms that light reveals (those forms being, for our eyes, the essence of light).

The human figure is a plastic form. The locus on which sound waves (through rhythm) and light rays (through the human figure) converge is the human body. Here is the mediating term, the incarnation, temporarily, of the god of song and light.

From an article in *La Vie Musicale,* Lausanne, April 1, 1908.

RHYTHM : ITS PLACE IN ART AND IN ACTOR TRAINING

As a corporal esthetic discipline Eurythmics will certainly have a great influence on the theatre, and it is interesting to try to see what the nature of that influence will be.

When I speak of "the theatre," I am referring to the auditorium as well as to the stage, to the audience as well as to the actor. Let us begin with the stage ; and since in Eurythmics music has the governing role, let us see what music is at present available to the actor for corporal expression on stage.

1) For light alone, with no obstacle to break against, we have, alas, only smoked glass...

In today's opera, which has reached a kind of apogee, the actor is indeed considered as the one who "performs" the action—he sings the text, and accompanies it with an appropriate set of mimetic gestures. Nevertheless, the actual dramatic expression remains enclosed in the score. Despite his singing and mimicry, the actor cannot definitively embody the dramatic expression. He goes painfully back and forth between two kinds of music. One expresses a thoroughly inner conflict, and cannot, therefore, provide him with subjects for plastic expression. The other kind of music does, on the contrary, call for strenuous outward projection ; but to the extent that it originates in the orchestra, it does not provide any greater number of patterns and rhythms that can be embodied by the actor. There are, no doubt, exceptions (more apparent than real)—and intelligent staging could, no doubt, improve this situation considerably. What results is nevertheless a simple juxtaposition between the music and the actor. *Organic* union remains impossible, for modern dramatic music is, after all, only the special development—the development to the utmost—of an art which has long since abandoned its relations with bodily form. Hence the inevitable mendaciousness of our operatic stage.

Modern opera is an extraordinary art, but it is already passé. We must, therefore, refrain from blindly applying to it the principles of an art that has not yet taken form, such as the one that Eurythmics is making ready for us. And in that case we may well wonder what use rhythmic gymnastics will be for our actors, since they find so little direct application for it on stage.

It goes without saying that if we inculcate rhythm into actors through some normal method and at the same time make them aware of the purely esthetic harmony of their bodies, that discipline will have a highly beneficial influence on their musical sense and musical qualities, as well as on the purity and appropriateness of their performance ; it will, moreover, bring them closer to a kind of moderation that borders on style. But this is a general consequence—one that has to do especially with restraint and a sense of music. It really belongs to the realm of actor training. We can do no more than mention it in passing, for what concerns us here is bodily rhythm.

It is true that in the theatre the actor finds no art equivalent to the one that introduced him to bodily rhythm ; he nevertheless does find one essential element that is common to both disciplines : *space.* The discipline of rhythm will have made him particularly aware of the dimensions in space that correspond to the countless varieties of musical sequences. Instinctively he will seek to make those dimensions apparent on stage, and at that point he will be forced to note with amazement the wrong that was done to him when he, plastic and alive, was placed in the midst of cut up, lifeless paintings on vertical flats. In regard to our operas too, he will feel the impossibility of any organic union between the set and himself. Again—a mere juxtaposition. He will realize that he is caught between two contradictions. One comes from a kind of music which he cannot embody but which he nevertheless has to "perform" on stage. The other comes from the so-called stage-setting—an aggregation of disparate elements which has no relation or contact with his plastic, mobile body, and which, consequently, is prejudicial to his working out any kind of rhythmic movement in space. The actor will thus become aware of the distressing role that he has been given to play. He will be able to stand up for his rights—*with full awareness of everything involved*; and he will thus be able to collaborate in the reform of drama and the stage on which we are—almost in spite of ourselves—already engaged. Eurythmics, by providing the actor with an *esthetic* education in the true sense of the word, will grant him that authority—and that is a consequence of inestimable value.

There is yet another personage on the stage, one who, though invisible, is nevertheless more genuinely present than anyone else—the author, the playright-composer. If he has experienced rhythm himself, if he has been able to note a spark of joy and beauty struck in the depths of his personality by the authentic embodying of music, then like the actor he will become aware that opera today—and consequently his own work—is only a discordant juxtaposition. Henceforth he will, on one hand, hear his music and, on the other, see his stage action; but no longer will he be able to confound the two as before. In carefully examining his memories of bodily Eurythmics he will rediscover in himself a harmony that he has lacked the knowledge and ability to create on stage. An unspoken accord will thus be established between the author and the one who performs his drama—the actor; both will *doubt* their work. Now, doubt is always the beginning of a search for truth. But how are we to reach that truth—that harmony ?

The author will not be able to delude himself for long. The present means of dramatic expression (score, actor, staging) have each developed independently of one another, and they have developed unevenly; anarchy has resulted. If we use those means of expression in the forms in which they are offered to us at present, we will not be able to make the slightest progress towards bringing about a harmonious collaboration among them. *We must change direction.* I am talking here about a conversion, in the most literal sense of the word. Music has long gone its own way. Neither by modifying it arbitrarily nor by imposing any arbitrary stylization on the inanimate equipment of the stage will we be able to bring music together with the living organism that is the actor. Here the conversion consists in a resolve to take *the human body* as a starting point, not only for music but also for all the stage equipment—ultimately, in other words, for our very conception of drama. And the conversion will also mean accepting all the consequences which that resolve will bring with it. No conversion is without sacrifices, and the sacrifices which this one will require are considerable. Above all it calls for complete unselfishness and total submission. The musician needs to retrace his steps and set out bravely in search of the body that he forsook centuries ago. Obviously the living organism must come to his assitance by providing him with an instrument that is ever more flexible, ever more attentive, and ever more aware of its latent harmony. The point of contact was lost. *Eurythmics seeks to rediscover it.* That is its fundamental importance for the theatre.

It remains for us to see what influence Eurythmics will have on the audience. That, along with the points I make above, will perhaps lead us to a new conception of the stage.

We may make this perfectly well-founded prediction : in the near future rhythmic discipline will not only be an integral part of the teaching given in our schools but will also be widespread among adults—sufficiently so for the theatre-going public to contain a high proportion of spectators who have been deeply imbued with it, or who have even had direct experience of it. What will their inner attitude be towards the productions they see?

Up until now, all we have asked of the audience has been to be still and pay attention. In order to encourage it in this direction, we have offered it a comfortable seat and have plunged it into a semi-darkness that favors the state of complete passivity which, it appears, is the audience's portion. That comes down to saying that, in the theatre as elsewhere, we seek to set ourselves off as much as possible from the work of art. We have become eternal spectators.

At that passive attitude rhythmic discipline strikes a staggering blow. As musical rhythm enters into us, it tells us, *"You* are the work of art." And at that point we do indeed experience the feeling, and will never again be able to forget it.

"This is yourself," says the Brahmin as he stands before each living creature. Henceforth, whenever we stand before a work of art, we will feel ourselves to be *ourselves,* and we will ask ourselves, "What has this work made of *me?"* Our attitude is changed. Instead of passively accepting, we will take an active part ; and we will have earned the right to rebel if we are forced to be untrue to ourselves. As for the kind of theatre we have been talking about here, it is perfectly obvious that the stage productions of the present day are perpetually forcing us to be untrue to ourselves. Anyone who experiences that violation in the manner we have just described will naturally revolt. Along with the playwright and the actor, he will doubt ; and along with the playwright and actor, he will seek truth *elsewhere.*

I am in no way overstating the case. The awakening of art in ourselves, in our bodily organisms, in our own flesh, sounds the death knell for a considerable part of the art of today, and for the art of the stage in particular. But so highly prized is the art of the stage as we know it, so vast a place does it occupy, that it seems we cannot do without it. With what, then, can it be replaced?

If the playwright and those who perform his work are to bring about a change of direction—a conversion—then the spectator must, in his turn, submit to it too. His starting point is himself, his own body. From that body, living art must radiate and spread out into space, upon which it will confer life. That body is what governs light and spatial balance ; it is what creates the work of art.

The transition will be slow, and from stage to stage it will call for a sturdy faith in the truth we have glimpsed. The Hellerau festivals will certainly constitute the most meaningful stage—the most decisive stage on the road to conquering a *living* art for ourselves. Each year they will bring together in a homogeneous fashion the exercises performed at the institute, presenting even the most advanced results of those exercises—and even grandiose attempts at dramatization. These *Festspiele* will be the performers' festivals. And the audience that is invited to attend them will be deeply aware of its feeling that these pupils—of every age and social origin—are assembled there *to represent the audience itself.* Like the ancient chorus around the lit altar, they will be the audience's direct and wonderful spokesman to living art.

And then, as the audience, full of gratitude, beholds them, it will—after so many centuries of isolation—be able to cry out :

"Yes ! That indeed is I !"

Our theatre will have been conquered for the audience.

As we see, Eurythmics and the theatre (the one we have at present) are two mutually exclusive ideas. By restoring the body to the place of honor, by accepting only what comes from the body or is intended for it, Eurythmics has taken a decisive step towards a complete reformation of our conception of drama and of the stage.

However, our present day theatres will exist for a long time yet. Thus, though the influence of Eurythmics will continue to benefit the actor and to inculcate a sense of stylization in him, we can predict that in our theatres Eurathmics will exercise its greatest influence on *staging.* Instead of a display of lifeless paintings on vertical flats, staging will come forever closer to the plasticity of the human body, so as to enhance that plasticity in space. From that a great simplification will result, and a notable diminution of the objects that only painting could show. Since the lighting will no longer be absorbed by the need to make painting readily visible, it will be able to spread out in space, imbuing it with living color and creating in it a shifting atmosphere with infinite variations—an atmosphere, moreover, which will work entirely to serve the dramatist rather than the scene-painter. As for the illusion that at present the painted set seeks to give us (to the actor's detriment)—we will, with the playwright's agreement, use it for the further enhancement of the actor himself. It is not possible here to go into further detail about the results of such a reform. One thing, however, is readily apparent. If we set staging free from the yoke of inanimate painting and the illusion it is supposed to produce—and if we thus endow staging with total flexibility and freedom—then, at the same time, we set free *the dramatist's imagination.* We cannot begin to appreciate the effects this reform of staging will have on the form of drama itself.

As for Eurythmics, by maintaining its basic scenic principle—to tolerate nothing around it that does not emanate directly from embodied rhythm—it will, through a normal progression, create a new staging for itself, one which will be a kind of necessary emanation of the plastic forms of the body and its movements as they are transfigured by music.

Then almighty Light will respond to music and enter into partnership with it. Light, without which there are no plastic forms ; light, which populates space with shifting gleams and shadows, which falls in still sheets, which gushes forth in colored, vibrant rays. In the light that bathes them in its invigorating atmosphere, bodies will recognize and salute *the music of space.*

For Apollo was not only the god of music ; he was also the god of light.

(Glérolles : April, 1911.)

"Rhythmic Gymnastics and the Theatre" ("La gymnastique rythmique et le théâtre"), in *Les Feuillets,* Geneva (February, 1912).

FOR A HIERARCHY OF MEANS OF EXPRESSION ON THE STAGE

If we are at present to make any judgment of dramatic art and the development of staging practices, we must begin with this indispensable idea : that there exists an interaction between the dramatist's original conception and the means he has at his disposal (and can count on) for performing his play. Obviously it would be more accurate to say that that interaction ought to exist, for today, alas, the determining influence comes from one side only—our modern conception of theatre and staging forces the dramatist to limit his vision. First of all, then, we will need to get some idea of that element that so tyranically bridles the playright's imagination.

The art of stage-directing is the art of projecting into space what the dramatist has been able to project only into time. Let us examine what our staging has to offer the playwright—and this mainly in Latin countries, where a predilection for the conservative (which sometimes plays a protective and salutary role) can, when living art is at stake, become a real danger. The first factor in stage-directing is the performer—the actor. The actor is the bearer of the action. Without him, there is no action, and consequently no drama. Everything, it seems, ought to be subordinated to that element, which comes first hierarchically. Now, the body is living, mobile, and plastic ; it has three dimensions. Space itself and the objects placed in it (which are intended for the body) will have to take scrupulous account of that fact. The general arrangement of the stage comes hierarchically directly after the actor ; it is the means by which the actor makes contact with stage space— the means by which he acquires his reality in space.

Here, then, we already have two basic elements : the actor, and the arrangement of the stage, which should be suited to the actor's plastic form and his three dimensions.

What remains?

Light.

Our stage is a dark, undefined space. Obviously, the first thing we need to do is see it. But that is merely a precondition—like the simple physical presence of the actor before he begins to act. Like the actor, light must become active. Now, the actor is light's hierarchical superior ; and if light is to rank as a means of dramatic expression, it must be put in the actor's service—in the service of the actor's dramatic and plastic expression.

Let us suppose we have created a space that suits the actor ; light will be under the obligation to suit both the actor and the space. We shall see the obstacle that our modern staging puts in the way of that. The flexibility of light is something almost miraculous. Light contains all degrees of brightness and movement ; like a palette, it contains all possibilities for color. It can create shadows, and it can spread the harmony of its vibrations out in space exactly as music would. With it, we control all the expressive power that is in space—if space is put in the actor's service.

Here, then, is our hierarchy as it should normally be drawn up :

The actor, who acts out the drama,
space, with its three dimensions serving the actor's plastic form,
light, which brings one and the other alive.
However... for there is a however, and you have guessed what it is : what about painting?
What do we mean by painting where the art of the stage is concerned?

A collection of painted, cut up strips of canvas, stood up perpendicularly and set out in depth on the stage, more or less parallel to one another. These strips of canvas are covered with painted lights, with painted shadows, with painted objects, with shapes, with architectural constructions ; and all that, naturally, is on a plane surface, for that is the nature of painting. The third dimension is insidiously replaced by a sequential— and mendacious—arrangement in space. Now, in the dark space of the stage, it is necessary to light this beautiful painting...

Let us imagine an art lover who placed his statues in the midst of sumptuous frescoes. If the lighting of the frescoes is good, what will happen to the statues? And vice versa.

Our staging has inverted the hierarchical order. Under the pretext of offering us a great number of subjects that are difficult or impossible to render in three dimensions, it has developed scene-painting to the point of madness, and has shamefully subordinated the living body of the actor to it. Light illuminates these strips of canvas (since we do have to see them) with no thought for the actor, who suffers the supreme humiliation of having to move among painted flats set up on a horizontal floor.

All modern attempts at reforming the stage concern this basic point—i. e., the manner of restoring to light its lost omnipotence, and thereby of restoring to the actor and stage space their full plastic value. If, then, our hierarchy is an inalterable reality—as it incontestably is—painting, the lowest ranking element, ought to be, if not sacrificed, at least made subject to the three other higher ranking factors. But by what means?

Let us not forget that here our concern with stage practice itself is only secondary. What we are after is the progressive re-establishment of an equitable reciprocity between the playwright and stage practice. Let us, therefore, go back to the playwright, and, through him, to our conception of drama itself. What we must construct is the future of the drama.

Our stage-directors have long sacrificed the living bodily appearance of the actor to the lifeless fictions of painting. It is obvious that, subjected to the tyranny of painting, the human body has not been able to develop its means of expression normally.

Today the return to the body as a means of expression of the very first order has taken hold of our minds. It has kindled our imaginations, and given rise to a number of undertakings which, though very diverse and, no doubt, of very uneven quality, all aim towards the same rehabilitation. Each of us, for one thing, has noticed that the performer has a tendency—an implicit one, so to speak—towards moving closer to the spectator; and as spectators, furthermore, each of us (some more deeply and enthusiastically than others) has felt himself somehow drawn towards the performer. Given the contemptible passivity that our theatrical productions require of us, we used carefully to veil this feeling in the darkness of the auditorium. Now, with the effort of the human body to rediscover itself, that feeling has practically become the beginning of a fraternal partnership; we would like actually to be that body which we behold. The social instinct, which up until now we have coldly repressed, has awakened in us, and the separation between the stage and the auditorium has become a painful barbarity arising from our egoism.

Here, then, is the key point for the reform of the drama. It must be loudly proclaimed: the playwright will never liberate his vision if he continues to see it as necessarily connected to the line of demarcation between the theatrical production and its spectator. That separation may be occasionally desirable, but it ought never to constitute the norm. From this it follows, needless to say, that the usual arrangement of space in our theatres should slowly evolve towards a more liberal conception of dramatic art. Sooner or later we will come to what will be called simply the hall—a sort of cathedral of the future, which, in a free, vast, and variable space, will play host to the most diverse activities of our social and artistic life. This will be the ultimate setting for dramatic art to flourish in, with or without spectators.

"Actor, Space, Light, Painting" ("Acteur, espace, lumière, peinture"), in *Théâtre populaire,* Paris (January-February, 1954).

LIVING ART

As I believe I wrote you, I am writing a new book this winter, around two hundred pages long and entitled *Living Art.* It will be a somewhat strange work, and it will certainly teach the reader a good many new things. It's in five chapters : 1) The Elements, 2) *Living* Space, 3) *Living* Time, 4) *Living* Color, 5) Collaboration (or Cooperation). Perhaps a sixth chapter too, that will be accompanied by a series of new drawings.

The three main themes—the especially interesting ones—will be, first of all, the technical part, where I *demolish* the myth of the coming together of all the arts—and where, in order to do so, I analyze each of our arts from that standpoint, showing the sacrifices that they have to make and the attitude that the artist in each of them needs to adopt if they are to earn their place in *living* art. Then the distinction between sign and expression—their inevitable alternation...

Finally, the necessity for actual life to have the collaboration of *living* art, which is not a personal product tied to a workshop. But how ? Etcetera, etcetera...

Two thirds of the work still speaks of theatre and dramatic art—*and* it's only in the last third that I can at last speak of the legitimate existence of the *work of living art* outside the idea of drama and as sufficient unto itself... Even without witnesses, without spectators... !

From this it will follow that dramatic art is to living art what industrial art is to the fine arts—that is to say, an applied art. I'm *sure* I'm right !

You understand no doubt. And that should please you. Or...?

Should the whole book be called *The Work of Living Art?*

That would be, it seems to me, anticipating the end, and then no one would understand the early parts.

I haven't yet got a publisher—and I don't know if I'll get one. Providence will be the judge.

Excerpt from a letter of Adolphe Appia's to Edward Gordon Craig, January 31, 1919.

SOME APHORISMS APPIA WAS FOND OF

"Man is the measure of all things." (Protagoras)

"The purpose of the work of art is to show some striking and essential quality—and therefore some important idea—more clearly and more completely than real objects do. To accomplish this, it takes a whole composed of interconnected parts and systematically modifies the relationships among them." (Taine)

"Music by itself never expresses the phenomenon, but rather the intimate essence of the phenomenon." (Schopenhauer)

Adolphe Appia
Sketches and photographs

LIST OF ILLUSTRATIONS

N. B. The photographs give a true reproduction of the deterioration that certain sketches have undergone.

1

3

5

6

11

13

14

15

16   clair de lune   L'escalier pourrait commencer plus à droite et monter plus haut

18

19

20

21

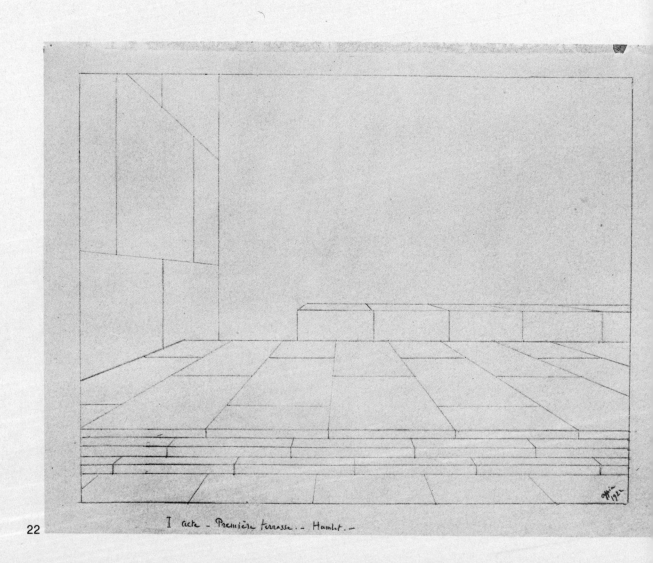

I acte - Première terrasse. - Hamlet. -

24

Adolphe Appia
1862–1928
actor – space – light

texts and captions
to the exhibition

Portrait of Appia at the age of twenty. (Private collection)

Panel 2

He is the one who, together with Gordon Craig, opened new avenues to us. He is the one who brought us back to greatness and to the eternal verities.

Appia was a musician and an architect. He taught us that musical duration, which envelops, governs, and regulates dramatic action, thereby engenders the space in which the dramatic action unfolds. For him the art of stage-directing meant one thing only : taking the inner shape of a text or of a piece of music and making it perceptible—through the living action of the human body and through the human body's reaction to the various resistances opposed to it by the volumes and levels (of height and of depth) built up on stage.

Hence the exclusion from the stage of all inanimate decoration and of all painted flats ; and hence the primordial role of that active element—light.

That said, nearly everything has been said. We have here a *radical* reform—Appia was fond of that word—the consequences of which, as they have been developed, go from Reinhardt's staircases to Russian constructivism. We are now in possession of a *given* of the stage. We can relax. We can work on the drama and the actor ; no longer need we walk a treadmill in endless search of "new" recipes for stage design or "original" methods of staging—a quest which led us to lose sight of our essential objective.

Appia's "given" is this : action in relation with architecture should suffice for us to create masterpieces—if directors understand what is meant by a drama and if playwrights understand what is meant by a stage...

Extract from an article by Jacques Copeau, in *Comœdia,* March 12, 1928.
The article contains a tribute from the founder of the Vieux-Colombier to the one whom he considered his "master."

A starting point:
Appia's thoughts on the contradictions of Bayreuth

Richard Wagner's ambition was for a "total" theatre, which would bring together music, poetry, architecture, gesture, and painting. He created the Bayreuth Festspielhaus (opened in 1876), taking his inspiration from the architecture of ancient Greece and Rome. But there were some conventions of his time that he was not able to get away from : the academic painting of the period, overloading the stage with ornament, the attempt to create illusion through the set.

The reality of the stage did not live up to his ambitions. He himself was to declare, "Ah ! I abhor these costumes and this greasepaint. When I think that figures like Kundry will be rigged out in fancy dress as if for Carnival... I created the invisible orchestra ; now if only I could invent the invisible theatre !"

In 1882 Appia attended the performances of *Parsifal* in Bayreuth. In 1888 he undertook *to reform stage-directing.*

The time was to come when, after having reflected at length on Wagner's work and having created numerous sketches for it, Appia was to write : "The master set his work into the conventional framework of his period ; and if everything in the auditorium at Bayreuth expresses his genius, on the other side of the footlights everything contradicts it." Adolphe Appia, 1925.

J. Hoffmann's sets for *The Ring* at the opening of the Bayreuth Festspielhaus in 1876. (Richard Wagner Museum, Bayreuth)

3/1 *The Rhinegold,* Scene 1.

3/2 *The Rhinegold,* Scene 3.

3/3 *The Valkyrie,* Act III. (Photograph of the designer's model.)

Panel 4

The Bayreuth Festspielhaus (1876).
Rising on the "sacred hill," the Bayreuth Festspielhaus did away with many of the structures of the Italian style theatre—there were, for example, no boxes
or horseshoe-shaped balconies. It attempted to
create "equality" among the spectators, and it made
the orchestra invisible ; but it emphasized perspective effects and maintained the proscenium arch. A
major innovation was that during the performance
the audience was plunged into darkness. The spell
of illusion was thus given free rein.

4/1 The ascent to the "temple."

4/2 The audience in 1876.

4/3 Cross-sections and plans for the building designed by the architect O. Brückwald, according
to Wagner's conceptions.

Panel 5

If the auditorium at Bayreuth was revolutionary, the
stage itself still belonged to the Italian style theatre,
then in decline. It made use of false perspective,
trompe-l'œil, and shaky painted canvas flats. Not
until 1952 would Bayreuth finally be rid of all that.

P. von Joukovsky, M. and G. Brückner :
The production of *Parsifal* that Appia saw at the Bayreuth Festspielhaus in 1882.
5/1 Sketch for Act I : the forest.
5/2 Sketch for Act II : Klingsor's castle.
5/3 Sketch for Act II : the magic garden.

The Rhinegold, or "the set and its gimmicks," 1896.
5/4 M. Brückner, sketch for the bottom of the Rhine.
5/5 Photograph of the designer's model for the pre-
vious set. (Theatermuseum, Munich.)
5/6 Stage photograph. The Rhinemaidens as they
appear to the audience. (Richard Wagner Museum, Bayreuth.)
5/7 The set seen from behind ! The trolleys built for
the Rhinemaidens by Carl Brandt at the end of
the nineteenth century. The handle was moved
up and down—while the trolley moved forward.
A crude method for giving the impression of a
swimming motion. (Credit as above.)

Panel 7

Appia's life and work : some dates

1862   September 1. Adolphe François Appia is born in Geneva, the son of Anna Caroline Lasserre Appia and Louis Paul Amédée Appia, the founder of the Red Cross.

1873-1879 Secondary schooling at the Collège de Vevey in Vevey, Switzerland.

1880-1888 He studies music in Geneva, Paris, Leipzig, and Dresden.

1882   Appia attends a performance of the original production of *Parsifal* at Bayreuth.

1886   He sees a performance of *Tristan and Isolde* at Bayreuth.

1888   Appia "resolves to reform staging and directing." (The words are Appia's own, from a curriculum vitae.)

1889   Stage-apprentice work at the Dresden Hoftheater.

1890   Stage-apprentice work at the Burgtheater and Hofoper in Vienna.

1891   "Withdrawal to the country in 1891 ; beginning of work in earnest." (Appia's curriculum vitae.)

1891-1892 Appia writes his "Notes for Staging *The Ring of the Nibelung.*"
He begins writing *The Staging of Wagnerian Drama (La Mise en scène du drame wagnérien).* First sketches for *The Rhinegold* and *The Valkyrie.*

1895   Publication of his first book, *The Staging of Wagnerian Drama* (Léon Chailley, Paris).

1896   Sketches for *Tristan and Isolde* and *Parsifal.*

1895-1897 Appia writes *Music and Stage-Directing.*

1899   *Music and Stage-Directing* comes out in German translation under the title *Die Musik und die Inscenierung* (F. Bruckmann, Munich). Not until 1963 will the work be published in the original French *La Musique et la mise en scène.*

1902   Appia writes "How to Reform Our Staging" (published in 1904).

1903   In May, at the Comtesse de Béarn's town-house in Paris, Appia directs the first scene of Act II of *Carmen* and a scene (the appearance of Astarte) from the Byron-Schumann *Manfred.*

1906	Appia discovers Jaques-Dalcroze Eurythmics and meets Jaques-Dalcroze. Their collaboration begins.
1908	He publishes "Notes on the Theatre."
1909-1910	He draws a series of "rhythmic spaces" for Jaques-Dalcroze.
1911	The construction of the Jaques-Dalcroze Institute in Hellerau, according to Appia's conceptions. Appia writes various pieces on Eurythmics.
1912	At the Jaques-Dalcroze Institute in Hellerau Appia does the stage design for the descent into hell from Gluck's *Orpheus and Eurydice*. He helps with the working out and staging of the Eurythmic exercices.
1913	Stage design for a full production of the opera *Orpheus and Eurydice* at Hellerau.
1914	Appia and Jaques-Dalcroze collaborate on the *Fête de juin* in Geneva. Appia meets Edward Gordon Craig in Zurich, where the two are guests of honor at the International Theatre Exposition.
1915	Octobre 28 : Jacques Copeau's first visit to Adolphe Appia.
1918	Appia writes the second preface to *Music and Stage-Directing* and, in all probability, the article "Actor, Space, Light, Painting."
1919	Sketch for *Echo and Narcissus,* which will be given in 1920 at the Jaques-Dalcroze Institute in Geneva.
1921	Appia publishes *The Work of Living Art* (Atar, Paris and Geneva). He writes "Stage-Directing and Its Future."
1922	Sketches for *Parsifal* (the magic garden), *Hero and Leander,* and *Hamlet*. Appia takes part in the International Theatre Expositions in Amsterdam and London.
1923	*Tristan and Isolde,* designed by Appia, is given at La Scala in Milan. The inspiration for the staging as a whole also came from him.
1924	The young director Oskar Wälterlin asks Appia to collaborate with him in putting on the entire *Ring* cycle at the Basel Stadttheater. However, the opposition of the self-styled "true Wagnerians" grows to such proportions that the theatre decides to forego the last two operas. Appia designs *The Rhinegold,* and stages it with Wälterlin's assistance.
1925	*The Valkyrie,* Basel Stadttheater, Appia/Wälterlin. *Prometheus,* Basel Stadttheater, Appia/Wälterlin.

1926	Sketches for *Orpheus and Eurydice, King Lear, Macbeth,* and *Lohengrin.*
1927	Appia begins a series of sixteen sketches for Part I of *Faust.* (They will be finished the following year.) He takes part in the Magdeburg Theatre Exposition.
1928	On February 29 Adolphe Appia dies in Nyon, Switzerland.

Giving visible form to «the work of Music»
The Ring (1892-1897)

Panel 8

"No musician excels, as Wagner does, at *painting* space and depth, in both their material and spiritual aspects... He possesses the art of using subtle gradations in order to translate everything excessive, immense, and ambitious in human nature and in the human spirit." Charles Baudelaire, 1861.

"... on stage we no longer wish to see things as we *know* them to be, but things as we *feel* them." Adolphe Appia, 1908.

Adolphe Appia, *The Rhinegold,* first version, 1892. Valhalla and its setting (as seen after Freia's exit). Autumnal atmosphere. (Collection suisse du théâtre [CST], Bern)

Panel 9

Adolphe Appia, *The Rhinegold,* first version, 1892. Valhalla and its setting. Valhalla itself—the abode of the gods—is in the background. (CST, Bern)

Panel 10

Adolphe Appia, *The Rhinegold,* second version, 1897. (Theatermuseum, Munich)

Panel 11

Adolphe Appia, *The Valkyrie,* Act III, 1892.
(Theatermuseum, Munich)

Panel 12

"Two radical reforms seemed absolutely indispensable to me : the role given to lighting and that given to the whole process of movement (vertically, and up and down stage). I mean that it was necessary to create an *atmosphere through the lighting and to make real use* of the set..."

"The sky is the center of interest up until Brünnhilde's entrance. At that point the focus of the drama shifts to a location which previously had served only as a kind of animated setting that commented on the action going on within it. But from this point on it remains—right up to the end—a living thing. We must treat it as such, therefore, and consider the lights and the other equipment as *actors* whose work in common has all the importance of a role in the drama." Adolphe Appia, 1891-1892.

Adolphe Appia, *The Valkyrie,* Act III, 1892.

12/1 The set (seen bare).
"The stage should give the audience a keen impression of a mountain summit... If the pine tree were shown whole, that impression would be destroyed ; that is why the presence of the tree is only indicated."
(CST, Bern)

12/2 As the curtain rises.
"Up until Brünnhilde's entrance, the Valkyries, who occupy the summit, play an exclusively decorative role."
(Oenslager Collection, Yale University)

12/3 "Wotan's impending arrival is announced by the approach of a fierce storm. The importance of the Valkyries recedes before the active role now played by the sky, on which they only comment." *"Der Sturm kommt heran./... Flieh wer ihn fürchtet !"*
(Theatermuseum, Munich)
(See the original on Panel 11.)

12/4 *"Weh !/Wütend schwingt sich/Wotan vom Ross !"*
(CST, Bern)
(See the original on Panel 13.)

12/5 Wotan bursts on stage.
"*Wollt ihr mich höhnen?/Hütet euch, Freche!*"
Here Wotan is center-stage. He will not move downstage until the climax of his dialogue with Brünnhilde. Then he will exit—in the gleam of the flames—by the narrow path leading up to the rocky summit.
(CST, Bern)

12/6 The stage after Wotan's entrance.
(Oenslager Collection, Yale University)

12/7 Wotan alone, center-stage, after his castigation of Brünnhilde, who is now asleep on the rock, stage left. "*Loge, hör! Lausche hieher!*"
(CST, Bern)

12/8 The stage just before the curtain falls.
(CST, Bern)

Panel 13

Adolphe Appia, *The Valkyrie,* Act III, 1892.
(CST, Bern)

The Ring (1924-1925)

From 1892 to the end of his life Appia made numerous drawings for stage settings for Wagner's work, particularly *The Ring, Parsifal,* and *Tristan and Isolde.*
During the first years his revolutionary vision was still marked by a desire for stylized representation rooted in what he himself described as "compulsory Wagnerian romanticism." With the passage of time—and after his experience with Eurythmics—his vision tended towards abstraction and geometrical formalization, even if in some cases Appia remained faithful to his early sketches.

Panel 14

Adolphe Appia, *The Valkyrie,* Act II.
Designer's model constructed by Harry Zaugg and Stefan Rebsamen from the reproduction of a lost

sketch. Stage space is reduced to a play of cubes and hangings. See the photographs of the 1925 Basel production (Panel 18, documents 3 and 4). (Pro Helvetia, Zurich)

Panel 15

Adolphe Appia, *The Rhinegold,* Scene 1, 1924.
The bottom of the Rhine.
(CST, Bern)

Panel 16

The Rhinegold : the 1924 Basel production, sets and staging designed by Appia.
(Theatermuseum, Munich)

16/1 Scene 3.

16/2 Scene 4.

Panel 17

Adolphe Appia, *The Valkyrie,* Act I, 1924.
Hunding's hut.
(CST, Bern)

Panel 18

The Valkyrie : the 1925 Basel production, sets and staging designed by Appia.
(Theatermuseum, Munich)

18/1 and 18/2   Act I.

18/3 and 18/4   Act II.

18/5 and 18/6   Act III.

Adolphe Appia, *Twilight of the Gods,* Acts I and II :
sketch, 1925.
(CST, Bern)

Panel 20

On account of Cosima Wagner's domination at Bayreuth and her fierce opposition to Appia's theories, it was not until 1923 that Appia was first given the chance—at La Scala in Milan—to convert his vision of Wagner's work into onstage reality. He was sixty years old.

"Bold attempts to break away from blind obedience to tradition and to put the characteristic forms of artistic expression of the twentieth century—expressionism, cubism, and abstract art—at the service of Wagner's work were attempted only in Germany and Switzerland—and not without being much decried and accused of politicization. It is really tragic for Wagner's work that Appia's brilliant desire for stylization did not suit the staging practices of municipal opera houses ; that the brave stagings of Klemperer and Fehling had to remain in the experimental stage on account of the development of the political situation in the thirties, so that their example could not spread beyond Berlin. It is tragic, finally, that Bayreuth did not begin until 1927—and hesitantly even then—to seek a compromise between Appia's conception and the conception of the partisans of absolute fidelity. By proscribing Appia's work *Music and Stage-Directing,* Cosima Wagner gave several decades' added life at Bayreuth to an artistic tendency that had long since become passé. In so doing she was acting against Bayreuth's revolutionary aims."

Wieland Wagner, 1959.

On February 13, 1894, H. S. Chamberlain, the author of several books on Wagner which had excited wide-ranging interest, wrote to his young friend Adolphe Appia :

"... all of your ideas are around seventy-five years ahead of the right time—the mother of the fellow who will get excited over your ideas is still a little virgin schoolgirl."

Little did he foresee that in the nineteen-fifties his own nephews, becoming the architects of the kind of reform that Appia so keenly desired, would create a "new Bayreuth."

Tristan and Isolde

Panel 21

"In *Tristan* Wagner allowed us to live the emotional life of his heroes more completely than in any other drama. But our eyes—to which appeal is nevertheless made—remain foreign to that heroic emotional life. In one sense, we 'see'; in another, we are only blind supernumeraries.

"The guiding principle for staging *Tristan and Isolde* consists, therefore, in giving the audience the vision that the heroes of the drama have." Adolphe Appia, 1896.

Adolphe Appia, *Tristan and Isolde*, the 1896 sketches. (CST, Bern)

21/1 Act II, Scene 1.

"The stage as seen when the curtain rises : a great torch shining brightly at the center of the stage-picture. The rather limited space that the stage reveals is illuminated by a diffuse light sufficient to make the characters perfectly distinct without diminishing the torch's somewhat dazzling brightness—and, most of all, without destroying the casting of shadows that comes from that brightness." Adolphe Appia, 1896.

21/2 Act III : Kurwenal's castle

"Except for the few signs indispensable for locating the action, the set for this act should simply enclose a sick man and a screen (with which Kurwenal tenderly protects his master and friend)." Adolphe Appia, 1921.

Panel 22

1923. Invited to direct *Tristan and Isolde* at La Scala in Milan, Appia returned to his 1896 sketches. In his new design, lighting still played a determining role ; but the set itself was less immaterial—less impalpable—and the lines of the stones were shown, albeit subtly.

Adolphe Appia, *Tristan and Isolde*. The 1923 sketches for La Scala. (Lithographic reproductions from the portfolio *Adolphe Appia,* Zurich, 1929.)

22/1 Act II, Scene 1 : the torch.

22/2 Act II, after Isolde has put out the torch.

22/3 Act II, entrance of the king.

22/4 Act III.
    The foliage of the tree from the 1896 sketches was replaced by a hanging onto which slides were projected.

Panel 23

Adolphe Appia, *Tristan and Isolde,* Act II.
Designer's model constructed by Harry Zaugg and Stefan Rebsamen from the 1896 sketches.
(Pro Helvetia, Zurich)

Parsifal

Panel 24

Adolphe Appia, *Parsifal,* Act I, 1896.
The sacred forest in front of the hall of the Knights of the Holy Grail.
(CST, Bern)
"In the music this forest represents a *temple.* It should have the character of a temple... The lines of the trees, therefore, and their general arrangement should be in conformity with this architectural kinship." Adolphe Appia, 1921.

Panel 25

Adolphe Appia, *Parsifal,* Act II, 1896.
Klingsor's castle.
(CST, Bern)
"The wicked magician Klingsor has built his castle on emptiness and the shadows of despair...
Singlehanded and mindless of the danger threatening him, Parsifal attacks the castle... Soon... the entire edifice collapses, giving way to the perfumed garden of living, musical flowers..." Adolphe Appia, 1921.

Panel 26	Adolphe Appia, *Parsifal,* Act III, 1896. The meadow in bloom. (CST, Bern)
Panel 27	Adolphe Appia, *Parsifal,* Act II, 1922. The magic garden. Final sketch. (CST, Bern)
Panel 28	—

Body, rhythm, space

Panel 29

In the spring of 1906 Appia attended a demonstration of Eurythmics by Jaques-Dalcroze. Filled with enthusiasm, he wrote to Jaques-Dalcroze almost immediately afterwards. "You will understand this enthusiasm better if I tender my profession of faith : through the *unrestrained development of its technical resources—* while the object of its *expression* remained *unchanged—*music has turned into something bearing a strong resemblance to self-abuse. Nothing but externalizing it can save it from this sumptuous decadence ; we must spread it out in space, *with* all the salutary limitations that that implies for it. Furthermore, the life of the body tends to anarchy, thus to ugliness. It is *music* which ought to free the body, by imposing its discipline on it. Your teaching makes music into something that affects the entire body, and thus solves the problem in the most practical way. You do not *make greater use* of the body and its posture ; you *seek* unity."

He had already had an inkling of this "rhythmic gymnastics," as he was to reveal in 1924.
"Already in *Musik und Inscenierung* I called for a kind of musical gymnastics, and wrote of it as indispensable for the actor of opera. But, obviously, I had no idea of how to proceed. Dalcroze showed me the way, and from that day on I have had a clear vision of the road my development should take. For me, the discovery of the basic principles of staging could only be a starting-point. Eurythmics determined my subsequent orientation. I was thereby freed of the restrictions attached to any particular, delimited work of art."
For Appia, Eurythmics was therefore a way of going beyond the drama itself ; it was a way to envisage a new organization of stage space. Indeed, in "Theatrical Experiments and My Own Research," Appia wrote the following :

79

"In the spring of 1909, Dalcroze asked me to attend a performance that he had carefully gotten ready, with original music, costumes, colored lighting, etc. I left the performance in sadness—and that decided me. I grabbed some paper and some pencils, and every day I feverishly drew two or three spaces meant for rhythmic movement. When I had twenty or so sketches, I sent them to Dalcroze, along with a letter in which I told him that his pupils, who were still moving on a plane surface, reminded me of mountain-climbers trying to climb the Matterhorn on a relief map lying flat on the ground !... His enthusiasm on seeing my drawings was very great, and I was convinced I had succeeded, as much for myself as for him. Henceforth, the style of space for bodily movement had a foundation. What remained was to try out that style in practice and adapt it, flexibly and undogmatically, to the needs of each new day. That required a good measure of feeling one's way ; and the staircase, which does so fine a job of aiding and abetting the body, became a reliable guide."
The drawings of rhythmic spaces dating from 1909-1910 are "meant for the creation of a specific style for the enhancement of the human body governed by music. They are not intended for anything else ; they are a starting-point." Adolphe Appia, 1921.

Rhythmic spaces

Panel 30

Adolphe Appia, rhythmic space, *Moonlight (Clair de lune),* 1909.
(CST, Bern)

Panel 31

Adolphe Appia, rhythmic space, *The Three Pillars (Les trois piliers),* 1909.
(Musée d'art et d'histoire, Geneva)

Panel 32

Adolphe Appia, rhythmic space, *Evening Round (La ronde du soir),* 1909.
(Musée d'art et d'histoire, Geneva)

Panel 33

Adolphe Appia, rhythmic space, *The Shadow of the Cypress Tree (L'ombre du cyprès),* 1909.
(Theatermuseum, Munich)

"For this space the artist had originally imagined an avenue of cypress trees. Little by little, he eliminated the trees, keeping only their shadows. Then, finally, this single shadow remained ; it is enough to evoke a whole landscape..." Adolphe Appia, 1921.

Panel 34

Adolphe Appia, rhythmic space, *The Clearing (La clairière)*, 1909.
(CST, Bern)

"Example of a forest simply suggested by strips of curtain and appropriate lighting... The light is muted at will by invisible cardboard cutouts, and the shadows falling onto the characters can thus become mobile. The fusion is total. The three tree-trunks in the foreground are probably superfluous." (1922.)

In 1902 Appia had already written the following :
"No longer will we seek to give the illusion of a *forest,* but the illusion of a *man* in the atmosphere of a forest... We in the audience will see Siegfried bathed in moving shadows instead of strips of cloth jiggled by strings..."

Panel 35

35/1 Adolphe Appia, rhythmic space, *The Last Columns in the Forest (Les dernières colonnes de la forêt),* 1909.
(CST, Bern)

35/2 Adolphe Appia, rhythmic space, *The Waterfall (La cascade),* 1909.
(CST, Bern)

Panel 36

Adolphe Appia, rhythmic space, *The Staircase (L'escalier).* Designer's model constructed by Harry

Zaugg and Stefan Rebsamen from the original 1909 sketch.
(Pro Helvetia, Zurich)

What is Eurythmics?

"To subject the human organism to the domination of musical rhythms and teach it to vibrate in unison with audible vibrations—that means freeing impulses that have long been held in check by the age-old defects of an education that has constantly restricted our underlying, natural instincts".
"Eurythmics orders our wills ; it establishes order, harmony, and clarity in our organic functions... It frees our bodies and minds from all harmful domination. Thus Eurythmics favors the natural development of our temperaments and insures the freedom of our instinctive rhythms."

Emile Jaques-Dalcroze

"To the individual who has been subjected to its discipline, rhythmic gymnastics brings the ability to understand the rhythmic organism comprised by a piece of music (even a very complex piece) and to give it spontaneous visual expression through gesture. Its end product is a sort of gestural music, which is even more interesting for the performer, who in performing experiences his full awareness of the music he hears, than it is for the audience merely watching a plastic representation of the music. Indeed, "representation" is too weak a term here ; we should speak of "incarnation" or "personification." The sense of the distinction is easy to see—we are not dealing with a diagram or lifeless figure, but with a sensitive, quivering organism.

82

And we are not dealing with any ordinary expressive material. The expressive material is the most beautiful living matter there is, the very model of plastic beauty : the human body. That is why Eurythmics is not a science but an art."

Ernest Ansermet

Panel 39	Adolphe Appia, rhythmic space, *Scherzo,* 1910 (CST, Bern)
	The inclined planes of this composition foreshadow "The Elysian Fields" that Appia was to design in 1913 for Gluck's *Orpheus and Eurydice* at Hellerau. (See the designer's model.)

Orpheus and Eurydice

Panel 40	Adolphe Appia, Gluck's *Orpheus and Eurydice,* The Elysian Fields. Designer's model constructed by Harry Zaugg and Stefan Rebsamen from the reproductions of lost sketches dating from 1912 and 1926. (Pro Helvetia, Zurich)
	"In a space like this, the procedure is naturally calm, without anything jolting. The soft, uniform, and slightly shifting light transforms the material reality of the construction into moving, gently rocking waves. Through the lighting, the characters share in this unreal atmosphere." Adolphe Appia, 1921.
Panel 41	Adolphe Appia, *Orpheus and Eurydice,* the descent into hell, 1926. (CST, Bern)
	This sketch harks back—but in a more realistic and monumental way—to the set Appia designed for the same scene at Hellerau.

Hellerau

In 1910 Wolf and Harald Dohrn built a full-scale cultural center for Jaques-Dalcroze at Hellerau, near Dresden. The *Bildungsanstalt Jaques-Dalcroze* was both institute and training-school. In addition to a huge theatre, it included such facilities as rehearsal rooms, a space for sunbathing and outdoor physical exercises, baths, living quarters for teachers and students, and a restaurant. It formed part of a vast garden city, the first on the European continent.

From October 1910 on the center was used for rehearsals ; the school actually moved into it at the end of 1911. Jaques-Dalcroze organized a series of festivals -*Festspiele*—to which those concerned with the arts flocked from all over Europe. At these festivals he displayed the results of his work through various types of presentations : exercises, demonstrations of Eurythmics, extracts from operas.

42a/1 The *Bildungsanstalt Jaques-Dalcroze.*

42a/2 The solarium.

42a/3 Ground-plan of the auditorium
length : 49 meters
width : 16 meters
height : 12 meters
audience capacity : 600

Panel 42b

"The theatre in Hellerau makes no claim to being an artistic salon, nor to being a temple like Bayreuth, but to being a *workshop*..."

Paul Claudel

A revolutionary theatre

– The audience is not divided up, but sits on a single bank of seats.

– Actors and audience are not separated by footlights, but are enclosed in the same space.

– There is no "set," but an acting area that can be shaped to fit the music—and the actors' bodies.

The Hellerau theatre, which helped point the way for the theatrical architecture of its period, was abruptly shut down by the Second World War.

Panel 42c

Stage and auditorium

It was Appia who, on meeting Jaques-Dalcroze in 1906, suggested that the bodies of the performers would be further enhanced if they were not on the same level as the audience. (At that time Jaques-Dalcroze was rehearsing in a simple hall, without stage or levels.) Appia also suggested that concentration would be greater if the Eurythmic dancers had constraints—material obstacles—imposed on them. He then had the idea of constructing staircases out of elements of standardized shapes and sizes—cubes and rectangular parallelepipeds that could be arranged horizontally or vertically, thus creating flexible acting areas that could be shaped to suit the choreography and staging of the exercises.

Today these elements (known in French as *praticables)* are perfectly familiar to us. Few of us realize that we owe them to Appia.

Another important element in this theatre was light. We have seen that beginning with his very first sketches, light had played a central role in Appia's work. At Hellerau, thousands of light bulbs behind the white curtains that covered the walls and ceiling produced a light that embraced everyone and everything.

Even if—contrary to Jaques-Dalcroze's wishes—Appia's name does not appear in the programs and is barely mentioned in the accounts of the performances given there, the Hellerau theatre is really Appia's.

"The theatre is a huge rectangle, with no fixed stage. The walls and ceiling are made of white cloth, behind which banks of electric lights are set out in a regular arrangement. No source of naked light is visible. All the lights are run from the back of the house by a console that allows a single person to create all the variations and all the different distributions of light and shadings that seem necessary. The ceiling, which breaks up into movable screens, more or less functions as a battery of light-projectors. Light is directed by that set of screens, and therefore acts as desired—either directly and transparently, or by reflection—and lends itself to every imaginable combination of intensity, movement, and direction. Instead of the brutal glare of the footlights, which flattens the actors against the backdrop and makes every stage picture into a gaudy tintype as discolored as it is loud, here we have a kind of milky, Elysian atmosphere that restores the third dimension to its neglected place of honor. It makes every body into a statue, whose planes, shadows, and reliefs are brought out and molded as if by the hand of some consummate artist. There too—just as music does in the Dalcroze method—light animates and brings to life the being whom it envelops ; it enters into collaboration with him. Light here is a creation animated by an unencumbered vitality—by higher order of life ; it is a far cry from the pale outlining of empty, painted simulacra that we are used to seeing on the stage."

"The Hellerau Theatre," from *La Nouvelle Revue française,*
for September, 1913. Unsigned article written by Paul Claudel

42d/1 Gluck's *Orpheus and Eurydice,* Act II, the descent into hell, 1912.
(Compare Appia's later sketch, on Panel 41.)

42d/2 The orchestra pit. It is in the middle of the theatre, and can be covered over. In the background : another arrangement of elements, probably for the Elysian Fields.
(See the designer's model, on Panel 40.)

42d/3 A demonstration of Eurythmics. The abbreviated costumes that Appia advocated were very "daring" for the period.

Opera and drama

Panel 43

Appia began with his thoughts on the work of Richard Wagner ; then came his experience with Eurythmics. He next applied to opera and non-musical theatre the principles he had learned : organize space, put light to work in the service of the actor.

Adolphe Appia, Gluck's *Iphigenia in Aulis,* 1926.
(Lithographic reproductions of the original sketches, from the portfolio *Adolphe Appia,* Zurich, 1929.)

43/1 Act I.

43/2 Act II.

43/3 Act III, first scene.

43/4 Act III, last scene.

Panel 44

Adolphe Appia, *King Lear,* 1926.
(Lithographic reproductions, as above.)

44/1 Acts I and II.

44/2 Act III.

Adolphe Appia, *Hamlet,* 1922.
(CST, Bern)

45/1 Act V, final scene, Fortinbras's entrance.

45/2 Act I, the guard-platform at Elsinore.

45/3 Act III, Elsinore. "To be or not to be."

Towards a new social art ; towards a new setting for theatre

Panel 46

The *Fête de juin,* Geneva, 1914

Appia was deeply affected by the 1914 *Fête de juin* ("June Festival"), for which he was one of the artistic advisers. In it, he discovered an example to "the work of living art" that went beyond the theatre proper.

"In Geneva, in July 1914, the first act of the *Fête de juin*—a great patriotic pageant commemorating the entrance of Geneva into the Swiss Confederation—gave a grandiose and thoroughly unprecedented example of this esthetic phenomenon. Jaques-Dalcroze, who composed and directed the first act, brought about the *simultaneity* of the two principles. At one and the same time the audience could see the acting out of historical events—the very succession of these tableaux constituted a majestic dramatic action—and their purely human expression,

46/1 During the last stanzas of an ode to the lake the light-colored curtains at the back of the stage opened, revealing the mountains and the lake, on which slender little boats were rocking gently. In the distance appeared the boat bearing the Swiss ; from this boat songs arose, which the Genevese took up in antiphonal response. The moment epitomized euphoric communion between peoples—their coming together in joy.

46/2 The Eurythmic dancers, dressed in sober gray tunics. They represent "the soul and feelings of the people." (Emile Jaques-Dalcroze.)
Here, "with grand gestures of taking the air," they dance the awakening of the City, while the Cathedral bells ring in the distance.

stripped of all historical apparatus, acting as a kind of sacred commentary on the events and transfigured re-enactment of them. This first act was a definitive revelation—achieved through the heroic courage and skill of the author and his collaborators." Adolphe Appia, 1921.

46/3 Here, they are "constructing the City" in a great outburst of communal enthusiasm.
(Photographs by Fred Boissonnas—Borel-Boissonnas archives, Geneva)

Panel 47

A new social art, a new architecture.

"Sooner or later we will come to what will be called the *hall (salle),* the cathedral of the future, which, in a free, vast, and variable space, will play host to the most diverse activities of our social and artistic life. This will be the ultimate setting for dramatic art to flourish in—*with or without spectators.* In no other art form can social solidarity be more perfectly expressed than in dramatic art. This is especially true if dramatic art returns to the greatness of its origins (transforming them after our own modern likeness)—origins which consisted in a communal attempt at giving perceptible reality to some great sentiment—whether religious, patriotic, or simply human." Adolphe Appia, 1918.

Panel 48

Drawing based on Appia's sketch : *Hero and Leander,* 1922.
(Pro Helvetia, Zurich)

No break between actor and auditorium ; instead, a unified space : *the hall.*

Appia's influence – The posthumous development of his work – His living presence

Panel 49

The history of the theatre is not limited to that of its most prominent personalities ; it cannot be summed up merely as the operation of esthetic influences. It is woven of a living material—the interchange between the audience and the varying action it sees on stage.

But it would be pointless to deny the real and often considerable role of those who at the end of the nineteenth century and the beginning of the twentieth attempted to rethink the theater, to work for a *new* theatre : Craig, Meyerhold—and Adolphe Appia, who holds a special place.

Adolphe Appia : a rebel and a thinker—but not a pure theoretician, as has too often been said. We hope that this exhibition has done away with that inaccurate picture.

Appia's vision had a profound influence on his own time (a time when the technical means available barely allowed for its execution) ; so deeply is his vision graven into our own age that we now tend to take it for granted.

As you look at these last photographs, you will see sets that sometimes imitate Appia's sketches and sometimes appear to be inspired by them ; you will see a light close to his, and spaces that give concrete embodiment to those that he imagined. This is Appia's *presence* today—in Wagnerian staging, in the structuring of stage space, in the creation of theatres where the dramatic act arises naturally in the midst of the audience.

But that presence must not be seen as a purely formal one. Rather, it is an invitation to understand Appia's teaching—one which calls for a theatre of rigor, on a scale and of a scope fit for man, that "measure of all things."

Wagner—from Appia to the new Bayreuth

Panel 50

Before the new Bayreuth

50/1 F. Kranich senior, *The Valkyrie,* Act III, the rocky summit of a mountain. Directed by Siegfried

Wagner, Bayreuth, 1930. Photograph of the designer's model.
(Richard Wagner Museum, Bayreuth)

50/2 E. Preetorius, *The Valkyrie,* Act III, Scene 1, directed by H. Tietjen, Bayreuth, 1935.

50/3 L. Sievert, *The Rhinegold,* a vast mountain site with open horizons, Freiburg im Breisgau, 1912.
(Institut für Theaterwissenschaft der Universität Köln)

50/4 L. Sievert, *The Rhinegold,* the appearance of Erda, Freiburg im Breisgau, 1912. (Credit as above)

50/5 H. Wildermann, *Siegfried,* Dortmund, 1920. (Credit as above)

Panel 51

The new Bayreuth : Wieland Wagner

"Today... electric lighting makes dramatic space, just as painting used to. Instead of an illuminated image, we have space become light." Wieland Wagner, 1951.

51/1 *The Rhinegold,* final scene, 1955.

51/2 *Parsifal,* the meadow in bloom, 1951.

51/3 *Parsifal,* the forest, 1956.

51/4 *Siegfried,* Siegfried wakes Brünnhilde, 1954.
(Festspielleitung Bayreuth)

Non-Wagnerian opera and non-musical theatre

54/4 FRANCE, 1921. Louis Jouvet, *La Mort de Sparte,* directed by Jacques Copeau, Vieux Colombier, Paris.
(Bibliothèque de l'Arsenal, Paris)

54/5 SOVIET UNION, 1922. A. Vesnin, *Phaedra,* directed by A. Tairov, Moscow.
(Theatersammlung der Nationalbibliothek Wien)

Panel 55

55/1 UNITED STATES, 1974. Josef Svoboda, *Sicilian Vespers,* directed by J. Dexter, New York.

55/2 GERMANY, 1922. T.C. Pilartz, *Oedipus,* directed by E. Keller, Darmstadt.
(Institut für Theaterwissenschaft der Universität Köln)

55/3 GERMANY, 1927. H. Heckroth, *Theodora* by G. F. Handel, directed by H. Niedecken-Gebhard, Münster.
(Credit as above)

55/4 SOVIET UNION, 1933. V. Ryndin, *The Optimist's Tragedy,* directed by A. Tairov, Moscow.
(Bakhrushin Museum, Moscow)

55/5 FRANCE, 1953. C. Demangeat, *Dom Juan,* directed by Jean Vilar, Avignon Festival, main courtyard of the Palais des Papes.
(Photograph by Agnès Varda, Paris)

New uses of space – new relations between actors and audience

57/3 ITALY, 1968. The Teatro Libero di Roma. *Orlando Furioso,* directed by Luca Ronconi, designed by Uberto Bertacca (Spoleto), seen here at the Halles de Paris in 1970.
(Photograph by Etienne George, Paris)

57/4 POLAND, 1968. The Cricot 2 Theatre. *The Water Hen,* production by Tadeusz Kantor, Cracow.